Two Dances and a Duke

Two Dances and a Duke

ELOISA JAMES

Acknowledgement

My books are like small children; they take a whole village to get them to a literate state. I want to offer my deep gratitude to my village: my editors, Leslie Ferdinand, Braden Mayer, and Anna Vettori; my agent, Kim Witherspoon; Jessica Mileo at Inkwell Management who worked with me on the Vella and print versions; my Web site designers, Wax Creative; and my personal team: Kamrun Nesa, Isabelle Guergolett, and Sharlene Martin Moore. My husband and daughter Anna debated many a plot point with me, and I'm fervently grateful to them. My heartfelt thanks goes to each of you.

Table of Contents

Chapter 1

April 14, 1814
Porterhouse Square, #38
Lord and Lady Sheffield's ball in honor of their daughter's debut

It was astonishing how easy it was to predict the future.

In a mere five weeks, Miss Beatrice Valentine had discovered that she had no need to gaze at the stars or into a crystal ball. She could make accurate predictions merely by peering at the ballroom from the shelter of a large fern.

Query: Will the lady dangling tangerine ribbons from her topknot drop her fan in front of the young man with the violet waistcoat?

Prediction: A probability of nearly 100%. The lady in question had already dropped her fan three times in front of various men, as if she were sowing a field and hoping a husband would pop up—a version of that Greek myth about sowing dragon teeth and harvesting a crop of Spartan warriors.

The lady's fan slipped from her gloved fingers at the same moment that Lady Sheffield's butler bellowed the names of new arrivals. The smile instantly fell off Bea's face and her heart started pounding in her ears so loudly that she couldn't hear whatever else he said.

She had thought that it was too late for new arrivals. That she was free for tonight. She never would have positioned herself so perilously close to the ballroom door, if she'd known guests might arrive so late, let alone these guests.

Bea swallowed hard. She would *not* disgrace herself by vomiting or crying.

Words to live by.

Her fern was no longer sufficient; she needed solid walls. A door with a latch or even better, a lock.

Their hostess, Lady Sheffield, rushed toward the ballroom entrance, her hand wrapped around her daughter Marguerite's forearm as she towed her across the floor.

When the lady slid to a halt, out of breath and full of apologies for dismissing the receiving line—though frankly, her guests were hours late—Lady Regina Charlotte Haywood, sister of the current Duke of Lennox, stepped forward and dropped a slight, if gracious, curtsy. Her fiancé, Lord Peregrine, bowed with the air of a man who didn't quite remember whose house he was in, and didn't give a damn.

In Bea's cynical opinion, Marguerite likely brushed her knees on the floor during her curtsy before Lord Peregrine. Rather than drop a fan, she gave him a long look at her cleavage.

Lord Peregrine's chiseled eyebrows twitched when presented with a pair of large breasts bolstered by short stays, but his expression didn't change. A housekeeper would look more excited glancing over melons for sale.

He was known as a rake, so perhaps he was bored by ladies' chests.

Still, Bea couldn't help taking a shuddering breath of pure longing. His cravat was crumpled, and his chin was shadowed—a terrible *faux pas* for a gentleman. He couldn't have made it clearer that he had no interest in the opinions of society madams.

Young ladies weren't supposed to feel waves of heat at the mere sight of a man's shoulders, especially those of bad men. Men with insolent eyes and a walk that wasn't a swagger but...

Bea couldn't quite explain it. When they'd first met, his eyes had skimmed over her as if she was invisible. A sensible woman would despise him merely for that. Still, she couldn't help thinking that perhaps Lord Peregrine was so bored because no one ever made him laugh.

Not that she was any good at making men laugh. But in her head, she was very witty.

Just then Regina's trilling laughter echoed around the ballroom. Bea's legs tensed with an impulse to flee, but she forced herself to take a deep breath instead. That would be foolish. Flight might attract attention.

Query: Now that Lady Regina has entered the ballroom, what are the odds that Bea's weight and unattractiveness will become a topic of conversation?

Prediction: Around 80%. Which meant there was hope, Bea told herself, fighting a wave of nausea. 20% was 1 in 5.

Her fern was leafy and tall, and she was tucked away at the edge of the room. What's more, Regina might be waylaid by a suitor hopeful of cutting out Lord Peregrine. As the daughter of a duke, and exquisite in the bargain, most of the available gentlemen in London had been at her feet until the evening when Peregrine kissed her hand, danced with her once, and told a friend he meant to have her.

At least, that was the gossip that Bea had overheard while lurking in the women's retiring room one night, confirmed by the fact their betrothal notice appeared in the papers the very next week.

Bea had felt sick with jealousy, but she understood. Regina was long-legged and thin, her body quivering with energy. She had a lovely face, if a rather predatory mouth. Yet to Bea's mind, the real appeal was that Regina wasn't docile and sweet, like most ladies tried to be. She was ferociously active, and "niceness" wasn't a quality Regina admired.

Neither did Lord Peregrine, obviously. They were well-matched, like eagles that would woo each other by dropping small dead animals in each other's path. Lord Peregrine clearly had no fear of competition. Bea had noticed his propensity to hand over his fiancée to any man who approached.

Regina had no need to drop her fan at the feet of another man should she wish for a different fiancé. If she showed the slightest interest, a suitor would likely drop to his knees.

But she never did.

Bea had discovered any number of parallels between ballrooms and barnyards, and Regina's behavior had a precedent in the hencoop. Regina had no interest in the rooster, so she was devoting her time to trying to plucking Bea's feathers, with the occasional sharp peck at other women in the vicinity.

From behind the shelter of a particularly large frond, Bea watched as a man she didn't recognize entered, joining Regina. She could only see him from the rear, but she didn't think she'd seen him before.

Lady Sheffield and Marguerite sank into synchronized, frenzied curtsies before him. What's more, Regina's closest friend, Lady Martha Telton-Sacks, burst from the crowd and sank into a curtsy, Misses Prudence and Petunia Massinger on her heels.

Bea shrank even further back behind the fern, cursing her bad luck. The depth of Martha's dip suggested that the stranger was Regina's older brother, the duke.

He was one of those eligible gentlemen whom her chaperone had warbled about introducing her to, which would frankly be a fate worse than death. Dukes were better than anyone at putting on a faintly contemptuous look that reminded an undesirable woman just how undesirable she was.

His Grace had just returned from somewhere. War? No, it couldn't be war. They never let titled men go to war, did they?

Prudence and Petunia were curtsying before him. The light of a chandelier directly above them made the twin's yellow curls look stiff and metallic. In fact, their heads looked like matching brass bed knobs.

Query: What are the odds that Prudence, Petunia, or Martha would marry Regina's brother, the duke?

Prediction: 70%.

Unless he was promised to another lady when he was in the cradle. Perhaps he was in love with a barmaid. Perhaps he planned to run away to sea.

Perhaps he was enamored of a footman (Bea's younger brother had returned from Eton with interesting facts that no lady was supposed to know). Perhaps he would be mowed down by a runaway horse before reaching the church.

In stark contrast to Regina's flashy elegance, her brother's tumble of hair was mahogany dark with a few lighter streaks, as if he had spent a good deal of time outdoors. Bea couldn't see his face, but even from here, she could see Prudence simpering and twitching her shoulders in a manner that suggested she found His Grace attractive.

Equally likely, she found his title attractive.

Query: What conclusion could be drawn about the Duke of Lennox, given his sister's character and his position in society?

Prediction: There was a 90% chance that he would be thoroughly despicable. To be avoided at all costs. Although the dowager duchess—

Bea let out a little shriek as acid peppermint-scented breath washed over her, and a fan sharply rapped her on the shoulder.

"I found you!" Her chaperone, Lady Alcon, was in a rage, not an unusual condition. She was a tall, lean woman who seemed constitutionally prone to either a twitter of nerves or a storm of bad temper.

"Straighten up, Beatrice," she barked. "It is extremely rude of you to make me poke around the ballroom, peering in the corners as if I were inspecting for dust. Lord only knows what our hostess thinks of me."

Bea dropped into a curtsy that was as deep as Martha's before the duke. "I apologize, Lady Alcon," she murmured, keeping her eyes on the floor. She had proved unable to disguise an ironic gaze around her chaperone.

Lady Alcon was not one to appreciate irony, and in a black mood, she tended to employ her fan until Bea's collarbone and shoulder were covered with little blue marks.

"I can't believe that you are hiding behind a plant like a lazy housemaid!" Lady Alcon went on. "It's quite intolerable that I keep having to search you out. Why, last Season—"

She broke off, likely because last Season didn't present happy memories. She had been given charge of Miss Leodoldina Cottons, who had danced with princes, flirted with dukes—before running away with a thirty-seven-year-old rake whose fortune failed to compensate for he twenty-year difference between their ages.

Miss Cottons' father had publicly blamed Lady Alcon for allowing his daughter anywhere near an aging roué, particularly a French one.

In the last five weeks, Beatrice had come to quite dislike Leopoldina without ever meeting her. In the normal course of events, Lady Alcon would have been shepherding about an aristocrat's daughter. But in the aftermath of Leopoldina's elopement, the lady had found herself available to chaperone a mere miss from the country, albeit one with a large dowry.

If Leopoldina hadn't made a cake of herself, Beatrice wouldn't be disappointing Lady Alcon on a daily basis.

Bea's father had been ecstatic when he managed to hire her ladyship. "I did inform her," he had announced, "that you were not to dance with any Frenchmen. Perhaps a German, but only if he had the best possible credentials."

Too bad that no one asked Bea to dance, French, German, or otherwise.

"I told you to keep walking," Lady Alcon snarled, pulling on Bea's arm. "If you insist on eating a meal before the ball, you must keep moving. Sit down for even for a moment, and you must ask yourself: 'Do I have the right to go into the dinner?'"

"I quite see your point, Lady Alcon," Bea said, planting her feet and staying precisely where she was, shadowed by the fern. Regina was turned away, which was a blessing, but if Martha glanced in this direction . . .

Martha was almost as unpleasant as her closest friend.

"My maid reported that you ate a large meal in the afternoon. Enough for two, and certainly not what any lady should partake in when she needs to look her very best."

Query: What is the likelihood that Lady Regina ate a meal before coming to the ball?

Prediction: Zero. Absolutely none.

Lady Regina was as lean and hungry as a whippet. Not a greyhound, because they were nervous but gracious. Whippets liked to bark.

"Although we both know the outcome of this Season," Lady Alcon said, "I shall still do my duty and introduce you to more gentlemen. *If you would stop hanging back like a sinner at the altar rail!*"

Query: What were the odds of Bea finding a husband during the Season?

Prediction: Again, zero.

This evening, for example, approximately forty young ladies were contending for twelve eligible gentlemen, although she might have overlooked an elderly widower or two, and she should add in the lame duke.

Even had she been as beautiful as Lady Regina, the odds were nil.

Fat ladies from the country weren't in fashion.

Chapter 2

When a person is discovered in a corner—hiding behind a fern, no less—that person should be left in peace.

At least, that's what Miss Beatrice Valentine thought, although clearly her chaperone, Lady Alcon, did not agree. "I can't think what you're doing here. I mean to introduce you to the Duke of Lennox, who just entered the ballroom."

"I'd rather remain in this corner," Bea said. Then, hoping for a reprieve, she appealed to Lady Alcon's encyclopedic knowledge of society. "Why would the daughter of a duke marry a mere lord?"

"To whom are you referring?" Lady Alcon asked, with an aggressive emphasis on grammar.

"Lady Regina and Lord Peregrine," Bea said. "He is not a member of the nobility, and obviously not an arbiter of society, as he doesn't care for his appearance, does he? So why did Lady Regina's brother accept his proposal?"

"Lord Peregrine is at the very top of society," the lady said acidly. "His dress is always *comme il faut*. His tailoring is exquisite, and the better for not being vulgarly colorful, like some fools."

"I see," Bea said, taken aback.

"What's more, his fortune is said to approach that of the Golden Ball," Lady Alcon added.

No wonder Regina didn't care about her fiancé's slightly contemptuous air.

"His fiancée has an excellent dowry," Lady Alcon continued. "She behaves just as a lady should. They are an excellent match. Her clothing, schooling, and manners are a credit to her parents, and were naturally rewarded by a match that equals hers in every way."

"Yes, I see," Bea murmured.

"You, on the other hand, are wasting your father's money," the lady said. "You are also wasting my time, but I am reconciled to that. You owe it to your father to try not to eat him out of house and home!"

"We could go into the far room," Bea suggested. "And please, Lady Alcon, could you keep your voice down?"

"I promised your father that I would introduce you to every eligible man in London, and that is just what I shall do. *I* do not shirk my duty, no matter how unpleasant. Come along!"

To Bea's utter horror, her chaperone jerked her from behind the fern and headed directly toward Regina and her friends—or more to the point, toward the Duke of Lennox. Bea's heart began beating fast in the base of her throat.

Bea couldn't break free and run, because Regina had seen them, and she was watching, eyebrow raised.

Earlier Query as to Bea's Weight as Subject of Conversation?
Probability: 100%.

Regina's remarks about Bea's body were like robins in spring: ubiquitous, flashy, and wholly impossible to ignore.

Lady Alcon thrust Bea in front of Regina's brother with an introduction that sounded like an apology. Bea took a quick glance at His Grace's eyes—they were the same color as Regina's—and barely managed to turn her shudder into a curtsy that suggested respect.

"Your Grace," she said, staring directly at the floor.

He briskly kissed her hand, bowed, and expressed something or other.

Lady Alcon had drawn Martha and the twins into a conversation, but Regina had attached herself to her brother's arm and was amusing herself by looking down her nose at Bea. It wasn't hard because Bea was, as her father used to put it, as small and round as an acorn.

The Season was only five weeks old, but she already knew what that smile on Regina's lips foretold. No need for a query; certainties weren't worth calculating odds.

"Goodness me," Regina said, her lips curling sweetly. "I do believe that you've been on a reducing diet since I saw you last, Beatrice. Don't you agree with me, Duke?"

Her brother, Bea saw with a fleeting glance, was glancing over the ballroom with the air of a man incapable of polite conversation.

Regina elbowed him, and Bea, watching the way the narrow point dug into the gentleman's side, was rather surprised when he looked down at his sister without indignation and said something in a deep voice that might have been, "Whoa."

In other words, the command one gave a horse when driving a buggy.

Regina's jaw firmed, but then she laughed. "You're such a charmer, Lennox."

"No evidence of that," her brother stated, obviously not giving a damn.

"Well," Bea said brightly, thinking that perhaps she could escape in the midst of a sibling squabble, "If you'll excuse me, I'll—"

Regina's hand whipped out, and she caught Bea's arm. "Oh, no! I insist that you allow my brother to share in your triumph, Beatrice."

Bea froze. What on earth was she talking about?

Regina turned to her brother. "Miss Valentine has put in so much effort to trim down all that flesh she carries around with her. You can see that she battles a morbid propensity to fatten, the poor girl."

A sickening heat swept up from Bea's chest into her face. "I don't battle," she croaked, which made absolutely no sense.

"It is so, so humiliating," Regina cooed, "but you are among friends here, Beatrice. My brother is always kind to those who can't help themselves. He's quite a saint, in fact. Just this afternoon he chided me for refusing a beggar." Her voice sharpened on the last word.

"It was less for refusing the boy than for kicking him," the duke said flatly.

Regina shivered in a dramatic fashion. "The rat dared to touch me, though he was dressed in the most revolting rags. I am certain that he was infested with all different sorts of bugs."

Query: What is the probability that a young beggar might transfer a flea?

Probability: Very low. Perhaps 5%?

One could always hope.

"You called me unkind, Lennox, but Beatrice can tell you that I have done my very best to help her from the moment she arrived in London."

"Help" was one way of putting it, if making Bea's life hell counted.

"I'm glad to hear it," Regina's brother replied.

Bea risked a look at the man. He was scanning the ballroom again, looking for a friend. Perhaps his mistress.

Having seen his expression, Bea predicted that even if Prudence curtsied so low that she plopped down to the floor on her bottom, this man had no interest in marriage or marriageable girls. The contours of his jaw were what one could expect from the aristocracy, but his eyes weren't. They were remote, chilly, and completely detached.

"Since I saw you three days ago, Beatrice, I trust that you have eaten nothing but potatoes and soda water, as I advised?" Regina demanded.

"Of course," Bea said, backing up a step and pulling her arm free. "I appreciate your advice."

Regina leaned after her, as if to share a confidence and hissed, "You didn't, did you? You look as fleshy as you did when I last saw you. Your face is as round as the moon."

"I did," Bea said.

A lie.

Regina saw it in her eyes. Bea had never been any good at lying.

"I think you need more convincing. Perhaps a touch of humiliation in front of the world will convince you."

"No!" Bea squeaked, but Regina's face twisted with disgust.

"You don't know what's best for you," she whispered, so sharply that spittle hit Bea's cheek. "Brother." Regina's voice was suddenly as light and airy as could be. "I insist, I simply insist that you dance with Miss Valentine."

Her brother turned back, looking down at his sister, one eyebrow raised. Bea shivered. If Regina's fiancé was perpetually bored, her brother was ... cold. Hard. Suddenly she did believe the rumor that he'd been to war.

"You know that it does remarkable things for a young lady's reputation to be seen in your company," Regina said, syrupy sweet.

The duke turned to Bea. "It would be my pleasure," he said. He flashed a smile, but his eyes remained arctic.

"No, thank you," Bea replied, keeping it simple. With an extreme exertion of will, she stopped herself from turning around and dashing into the crowd. When, oh when, had she become such a coward?

It was just that Regina was looming over her. Why did the woman have to be so confounded *tall*? If Regina wasn't so big, Bea would be better at fighting back.

At least, that's what she told herself.

Bea never realized before coming to London that she was such a craven, chicken-hearted fool. She dropped an awkward curtsy. "If you'll excuse me, I have to—"

"No," Regina stated. "Lennox, just look at what you've done! You've frightened poor Miss Valentine with your ghastly lack of courtesy. Shame on you, Brother. I *insist* that you take Miss Valentine onto the ballroom floor."

"No, please!" Bea exclaimed, but Regina spoke over her.

"Dancing with a duke will cause all eyes to be on Beatrice. It might be just the thing to bring her into fashion. We've been trying to get people to stop saying such unkind things about . . . well, about her figure, but to no avail."

The duke cast his sister a look that—surely that wasn't dislike? No; there was no emotion at all in his eyes. He reached out and took Bea's hand before she could snatch it away, bowed, and brought it to his lips. "I repeat that dancing with you would be a pleasure, Miss Valenthorn."

"Valen*tine*," she said, rescuing her hand.

"Of course."

"Thank you, Lennox," Regina said, beaming. She turned to Bea. "You probably don't realize this, having spent your life in the country, but my brother doesn't dance with just anyone. You'll want to be your most graceful, Beatrice."

The duke caught that and frowned at his sister. "Of course Miss Valentines will be graceful."

"Valen*tine*," Bea said, but she kept it low. Perhaps he was mispronouncing her name to make fun of her. That was precisely the sort of foolish quip that sent Regina into trills of laughter.

"You have no need to remind the lady to be poised," His Grace finished.

Bea was graceless on the dance floor, and Regina knew it—which was precisely why she had pushed her brother into the dance.

Bea invariably turned the wrong direction and couldn't seem to remember the pattern. Waltzing was a particular horror. The men were all so tall that she found herself being jerked along, like a marionette on strings.

"They're calling a waltz!" Regina cried, clapping. "Now remember, Beatrice. Follow the duke, and don't try to take control, the way you did with Lord Fettle. We all know *that* didn't end well."

Fettle had been drunk, tripped over Bea's feet, and bumped into Regina. Regina had given Bea a shove that sent her sprawling on the floor.

That was the first time she came to Regina's attention, five wearisome weeks ago. Fettle had capped the event by laughing hysterically when Regina had surveyed Bea and announced to all and sundry that Bea's tumble was clearly due to the fact that her weight made her unsteady on her feet.

"Of course, Lady Regina," Bea said woodenly. Her heart was beating so fast that she felt light-headed.

There was no escaping it. Naturally, Lady Regina's brother was the size of a mountain. If she ever met a gentleman whom she could contemplate marrying, he would have to be a reasonable size.

Not outlandishly large, with shoulders to match.

Not that she would ever consider a duke. She had a precise understanding of her worth, thanks to the last five weeks. She would never set her sights as high as a duke.

In fact, Regina and her friends didn't even think Bea was worthy of a gentleman. Martha had remarked that Bea would be best paired with a butcher or a baker, someone who could feed her appetites.

All she wanted was a reasonably-sized man with kind eyes.

She pushed the thought away. Dancing would get her away from Regina. All the way to the other side of the ballroom, in fact. She merely needed to think of it as an escape, rather than a humiliation. "Your Grace," she said, curtsying before the mountain.

"Miss Valentines," he said, bowing yet again.

Chapter 3

Miss Beatrice Valentine may not have danced with many dukes—in fact, this was her first—but she knew that the rules of polite society dictated that she shouldn't insult the Duke of Lennox by disagreeing. For example, by pointing out (again) that her last name wasn't Valentines, but Valentine.

The only thing on Bea's mind was getting through this bloody dance and running for the ladies' retiring room—obviously, the fern she had hidden behind earlier had been inadequate.

She would allow His Grace to waltz her just far enough away so that she could escape. Behind her shoulder, Regina, Matilda, and the twins were tittering loudly at the idea that *she* was to dance with a duke.

Query: What are the odds this man would have the same character if he were born a peasant or a grocer?

Probability: Zero.

He was monstrously tall, but it was the unpleasant eyes that really betrayed his rank. She liked warm blue eyes. His were like a snowy field at twilight: gray and treacherous. Just like his sister's.

The strains of a waltz began. The duke was so large that she had to stretch to reach his upper arm.

"All right," she murmured, so quietly that her lips scarcely moved, "just…just get through it."

"Excuse me. I didn't hear you. What did you say?" His Grace asked. He took her right hand in his. To his credit, he didn't pull her arm to an uncomfortable height.

She didn't look up or answer his question; it would just encourage him to make fun of her. Give him ammunition to share with Regina.

True, the siblings didn't seem to like each other, but that was the way of vicious creatures forced to grow up in the same den. She'd read about the habits of the African animal called the hyena, for example. Siblings regularly ate each other.

"Miss Valentines?" he asked, with just the faintest intonation that suggested he wasn't used to being ignored.

"My name is *Valentine*," she said, taking a breath. Her pulse was still racing, even though they were moving toward the edge of the dance floor. Sad though it was, with every inch of distance gained from Regina, Martha, and the rest she felt braver.

She was still a pitiful coward, though, given that she desperately wanted to run out the door.

"Please forgive me," the duke said, sounding completely unmoved by regret. "Miss Valentine."

As the music began, Bea reminded herself to follow his lead. To step widely because his legs were so long. To be light on her feet and—

While she was still reminding herself of the rules for dancing with monstrously sized men, they reached the edge of the dance floor and began. The duke held her so steadily that after a moment she forgot about taking wide steps.

In fact, their feet moved perfectly together, in tune with the music. Before Bea realized what was happening, he turned her in a smooth circle. Out of the corner of her eye, she saw her gown float out behind her. She'd only seen that happen when other girls were dancing.

Pretty girls, like Martha, Petunia, Prudence and Regina.

The duke seemed to know instinctively when another couple was veering close to his back. He would quickly correct their course, turning Bea in a gliding circle.

"You said something that I missed," he said, after a few more moments of dancing.

For goodness' sake, he was persistent. Did they really have to converse? Wasn't being forced to dance with a short woman whom he didn't even know punishment enough for him?

Bea forced her lips into a smile and looked up. "I said nothing important, Your Grace."

Hooded gray eyes were gazing down at her without the appearance of mockery. "My sister is not always kind, but it seems she has taken a genuine interest in you. Yet you looked pained as we began dancing. I hope that you weren't insulted by her eagerness to see you show yourself to advantage on the floor. Obviously, she had no idea how graceful you are."

Graceful? Bea could have snorted, and Regina definitely would have done so. Yet the duke was an astonishingly good dancer. Every other man she'd danced with had made her feel like a round pumpkin paired with a corn plant, but the duke seemed to instinctively move with her. This was ... *fun.*

"I'm honored by Lady Regina's interest," Bea said hastily, realizing she hadn't answered his comment. She failed to make the sentence sound even slightly convincing, which was frustrating. Everyone else seemed to be able to fake their emotions.

Her life with Lady Alcon would be a great deal easier if she had better control over her expressions.

Query: Would relations with Regina be better if she were able to offer lavish, if false, compliments?

Probability: Perhaps 50%?

Offering a compliment seemed quite likely to drive Regina to further heights of unkindness.

The duke's brows drew together slightly, and he gave her a searching look. She immediately dropped her gaze to his shoulder, willing him to keep silent. Couldn't she just enjoy this dance?

She might never dance with this particular duke again, and she was determined to savor it. The music sped up; now it sounded like tumbling water. Their arms held wide, His Grace began turning her again and again. Her dress was floating, and Bea felt light on her feet.

She couldn't stop herself from smiling; it felt as if the music was flowing through her to the tips of her fingers, as if she were a fluffy seedpod spinning on an eddy of wind.

If she found a husband someday, she would teach him how to waltz properly with a short woman like herself. Most men held her awkwardly, hunching their shoulders, or dragging her arm half out of its socket. But the duke made it easy.

"I gather this is your first Season, Miss Valentine?" he asked.

"Yes, it is," she answered.

She was trying to ignore him and concentrate on the music. It wasn't easy, though. The duke smelled so good, a blend of sandalwood, leather, and fresh, clean laundry.

She would insist that her husband—grocer or no—change his clothing every day, she thought dreamily.

The music sped up again, and His Grace swept her in one circle, then another, and another. It was so joyful that laughter burst out of her before she could stop it.

There was something sober and dark-edged about the duke's face. But his mouth eased in response to her laughter. "You like to turn?"

"Yes!"

Nodding, he whirled her again and again, so quickly that everyone around them turned into a blur. Bea had no idea whether people were laughing at her, but for the first time since she came to London, she didn't care.

Elation forced away the humiliation and disappointment she'd been soaking in.

Alas, the tempo finally slowed, and so did they. "You're a marvelous dancer," he said.

"Pish," Bea said, when she had caught her breath. "I'm a rotten dancer, Your Grace. I am merely lucky enough to be partnered with you."

She was morbidly aware of her ragged breathing. He was likely thinking that it was due to her extra girth. It wasn't, it really wasn't: Bea could ride for hours. But dancing with a duke? Spinning in circles and feeling like Cinderella, stealing her hour of happiness at the ball?

It took her breath away, just as it would any silly girl who dreamed of becoming a duchess. That was such an appalling thought that she dropped his hand as if it were a cold slug. Not only was she uninterested in being a duchess, but she was acutely aware that this particular duke would never seek her out, shoe in hand.

Query: The likelihood that the duke will ask her to dance again?

Probability: Zero.

His Grace hadn't even asked her *this* time; Regina had forced the issue.

"In fact, you are one of the best dancers I've ever partnered," His Grace said, voice low and thoughtful.

Bea's mind registered those words slowly. Just by dancing with him, she knew that he was a man of ruthless purpose. He would never lie; he wouldn't bother.

Then she became aware that ragged breathing was causing her bosom to ... to *heave*. His eyes hadn't strayed below her chin, but he knew.

Of course, he knew. The expression in his eyes was pure, sensual masculinity, distilled.

Surely, he realized that gentlemen didn't look at her this way. She was the opposite of desirable. She dropped into a curtsy, and as she rose, politeness demanded that she meet his eyes once again.

He was looking at her with a wary, puzzled expression. Perhaps he was shocked that she hadn't tripped him up and fallen to the ground.

"Good evening, Your Grace," she said. Then she turned and walked away, which wasn't entirely polite. He was supposed to escort her back to Lady Alcon, but she had a feeling that his training would insist that he murmur something about partnering her again at some point.

No.

She had to excise him from her mind. That dance was—

Magic. And over.

It was over.

Query: Does a duke think about a plump partridge from the country after his sister forces him to dance with her?

Probability: Too depressing to put into numbers.

Chapter 4

April 15, 1814
The Saville Club
69 Brook Street

"Lennox! Prinny wants everyone to go to the Pantheon now." Lord Devin erupted into the library of the Saville Club. "There's a troupe of Russian opera dancers dressed like daisies who've lost most of their petals, and he wants to pick some flowers."

Jonah Cecil Crawford Lloyd—also known as the Duke of Lennox—didn't turn from the window, just shook his head. "Can't. I have to go to Almack's Assembly Rooms for a few hours at the least."

"Where bachelors go to die?" Devin snorted. "You're not thinking about taking a wife, are you? Does grief have you lurking in the library like some great raven?"

Jonah turned on his heel and surveyed his best friend. They were both blessed with freakishly large shoulders, but Devin was wearing an elegant violet-colored coat hemmed with embroidered silver scallops studded by pearls. "I'd rather be a raven than a peacock in that coat."

Devin chuckled. "I look *au courant*, whereas you look like the vicar. This Season, coats are cut short, with the tails to the back of the knee. Yours is about as fashionable as a cassock."

Jonah shrugged. "You're wearing knee breeches, so you can accompany me to the assembly rooms. You can peacock around the ballroom, showing off your exposed belly."

Devin's thick brows drew together. "Absolutely not. Almack's is swarming with marriageable girls determined to attach themselves to my arm, demanding a ring."

"My sister is one," Jonah remarked.

He saw his comment register in Devin's eyes. "Of course," his friend said hastily. "The beautiful Lady Regina. Just so! I'm shocked I forgot. Debuted a few weeks ago, didn't she? No offense, I hope?"

"None taken."

"I'm not concerned about marriage yet," Devin added. "If I was, I'd be joining the men at her feet, no doubt."

"No, you wouldn't."

"What?" Devin was frowning again.

"You're my friend," Jonah said, keeping it simple. "I wouldn't wish Regina on my worst enemy. Also, she's betrothed, thank God. Peregrine took her on. My father set it up before he died."

That brought one of Devin's barks of laughter. "I used to feel that way about my older sister. Now that she's married and has two children of her own, it's all different. I find myself looking forward to supping with her on Sundays."

Jonah thought about clarifying his feelings toward Regina, but what was the point? She had a fiancé. "I didn't realize you were coming here tonight."

Devin slung an arm around Jonah's shoulder. "After the way I pummeled you this afternoon, I thought I should check on your health. It's my Christian duty, although I didn't know you intended to continue to Almack's. Accompanying you there would be the action of a saint, not a mere Christian."

Jonah snorted. "You pummeled me? I remember pulling you up from the mat as weak as a newborn babe."

"You have a punishing right arm," Devin agreed. His easy grin acknowledged the fact that the two of them were evenly matched, as well they should be, since they'd been boxing together since they were youngsters. "I suppose I could come with you to Almack's for a few hours, if you'll come to the Pantheon after."

"I must wait until the supper dance," Lennox said. "I'm taking in Regina."

"Why haven't you handed your sister over to a female relative?"

"She has a chaperone, of course. But I try to accompany her the way my parents would have."

His answer had nothing to do with that young lady he met. Beatrice Valentine, his sister's—

No. Nothing to do with her.

"Are you planning to dance with anyone other than your sis?" Devin continued, walking over to the sideboard and pouring himself a drink. "You do know that every time you dance with a lady, they add her name to the betting book in White's, don't you? The duchess sweepstakes are growing larger by the moment."

"Regina told me as much. I promised I'd join her there, but that doesn't mean I have to dance."

"You should dance with the whole lot of them," Devin said, his eyes glinting over his glass of brandy. "Set the dowagers into a frenzy of speculation."

"Why would I do that?" Jonah inquired.

"You have to marry at some point," Devin pointed out. "If you're determined to go around with your sister, you should get something out of it. Wrap up the business of finding a wife."

It wasn't an entirely stupid idea. He needed an heir, as he'd be damned if he allowed the estate to fall into the hands of his cousin, who was a piss-poor judge of character and a gambler to boot.

Not when he was spending every possible hour mending the damage his father's reckless behavior had caused.

But take a bride? The idea was stomach-churning. He didn't like the girls one was supposed to marry. They wielded nasty words like assassins' blades.

He tolerated it in his sister Regina because what else could she do? Powerless people fought for the little power they had, like dogs over scraps. They battled for the power of a title, and "duchess" was a very great title, as those things went.

"You went to the Sheffield ball last night, didn't you?" Devin asked.

Jonah nodded.

"Did you dance with anyone?"

Once again Miss Valentine's clear eyes came back to him. She had spoken to him as if his title didn't exist. Twice he saw a flash of scorn in her eyes, though most of the time she looked at his shoulder, not his face. And then when she laughed—

"Once, upon the request of my sister," he replied. "I spent the rest of the night in the card room."

"You can't do that," Devin said, scowling at him. "If you don't dance, you're supposed to keep an eye on your sister. Stay in the ballroom."

Jonah loathed the conversations that happened at balls. It wasn't merely because he couldn't hear from his left ear after being deafened by cannon fire, either. He didn't like the sort of things that were said. The cruelty, the gossip, the foolishness.

"You should stay in the same room as your sister at all times," Devin stated.

They'd been friends for most of their life, but Jonah sometimes thought that they were a different species. Devin was sunny, charming to everyone he met. Full of goodwill.

"The hell I will," he retorted. "I hired Mrs. Hastings to chaperone her. As I see it, I take my sister to market—"

"That's a damned denigrating thing to say about your own sister," Devin said sharply.

"You think I mean so that men can look her over?"

Devin frowned at him.

"It's so that *she* can look over the men on offer, you ass," Jonah said. "Regina doesn't need advice from me."

"That's what you think," Devin said. "One of my sisters almost eloped with Rothingale."

"That fool?"

"Yes, but he wears a coat to advantage, and all her friends thought he was handsome, or so she admitted later. You have no idea how influential clusters of women can be. They talk each other into any manner of idiocy."

Jonah hadn't danced with a woman in ages, knowing how people would start twittering about his dance partner. Except for Beatrice. Miss Valentine. No, Beatrice . . .

He would never marry one of his sister's friends, no matter how her joyful laughter had fired his belly.

There was something shocking about Beatrice Valentine. She was delectable, plump, and curving in all the right places, her hair glossy and soft looking, her lips pillowy.

She was sensual, the way an opera dancer is sensual, with the kind of body that makes a man's jaw clench. He was surprised that Miss Valentine hadn't many suitors, at least according to his sister.

"If you're going to Almack's in place of your mother, you cannot hide away," Devin was saying. "You're like a male version of a wallflower."

"I don't know why not," Jonah retorted. Last night he'd had an uneasy sense that if he returned to the ballroom, he might make a fool of himself by searching out Miss Valentine.

God knows, he couldn't ask a woman to dance with him twice. It was tantamount to asking her to marry him.

"You must ensure that Lady Regina is not making irresponsible decisions," Devin responded. "I have four sisters, so trust me on this. They can get into trouble before you blink an eye, whether they're betrothed or not. It's her first Season, so she's sure to put a foot wrong."

Jonah managed not to snort. Regina had been breaking hearts since she was thirteen years old. He pitied Lord Peregrine. He didn't know what hit him, the poor sod.

"Did you even dance with your sister last night?" Devin said, scowling.

Jonah only danced with Regina when she commanded it. "No."

"You have to look at her dance card and cross off any bounders who managed to sneak their way on. She's a duke's daughter, you idiot. She's prey to any number of fortune hunters."

No, she wasn't. Or if she was, they'd back away slowly once they got a closer look at the miracle that was his sister.

"All right, I'll do it for you," Devin said, rolling his eyes. "I'll dance with her, ask to see her card, and cross out any man she shouldn't dance with."

"No!" Jonah snapped, not thinking. "Stay away from her."

Devin's mouth curled into a smile, but years of friendship told Jonah that his friend was offended. There was just the faintest shade of injury in Devin's eyes.

"I wouldn't want my sister dancing with me either," he said lightly.

True, Devin was a rakehell and had been since the age of eighteen. But he was also rich as Croesus; his father had so much money over and above the entailed estate that he'd endowed all his children with a duke's ransom.

That was one of the things that had bound Jonah and Devin together as children. They knew what it was to grow up amid extreme wealth and discover it's a hindrance to becoming a man. Though one signal difference was that Devin's father was devoted to growing his estate and Jonah's father to wasting his.

"Nothing to do with your reputation. You don't understand."

"I do." Devin's eyes were perfectly sunny. "I have four sisters. I don't know that I'd want you to marry one of them, either."

"Damn it." Jonah wrestled with the right words, but Devin was already at the door.

"If I'm not reviewing Regina's dance card, then you must. You'll have to be on duty the rest of the Season."

"As I said, she has a chaperone," Jonah said.

Devin shouldered open the door. "She's your little sister," he said impatiently. "You need to guide her choices."

The man didn't have the faintest idea what he was talking about.

Chapter 5

April 15, 1814
Almack's Assembly Rooms
South King Street

*A*lmack's Assembly Rooms…The dancing hall every young lady dreams of entering. The place that issues vouchers for entry, allowing only the *crème-de-la-crème* to walk through the door. The place where matrons rule, and gentlemen must wear knee breeches. Where the lemonade is warm and the ham sandwiches thin.

The place that Beatrice Valentine dreaded even more than ballrooms. Balls took place in houses with rooms and curtained alcoves in which one could hide. An assembly hall sounded bare. Frankly, she had been happy when Lady Alcon moaned about the fact Bea hadn't been given a voucher to Almack's.

Until the voucher arrived that morning.

"Don't forget to be on your best behavior," Lady Alcon hissed, as they climbed out of the carriage. "I don't want to have to nose you out of a corner like a hound after a fox. Not here, in Almack's."

Bea would have liked to disclaim this unpleasant description, but it was true. She went to ground whenever possible, after which Lady Alcon rooted her out like a pig with a truffle. She kept that reflection to herself.

"I'm so grateful that we received your voucher," her chaperone said, her tone making it clear that she was also quite shocked. "Lady Regina's kindness in forcing her brother to dance with you may have turned the tide of your fortunes!"

She'd only made that remark three or four hundred times since breakfast. Lady Alcon seemed to have missed the signal point that Bea would never have received a voucher if Regina had anything to do with it.

Lady Alcon gave her a commanding stare as they handed their pelisses to a footman. "You acquitted yourself decently on the dance floor with the Duke of Lennox, so you can do so with other men as well. I don't want to see you flailing about like a trout on a line."

Bea nodded.

Query: Would Lady Alcon ever give her a true compliment?

Probability: 20%?

She'd come close to it after Bea's unexpectedly successful dance with the Duke of Lennox: her chaperone had described her comportment as "nearly elegant."

Lady Alcon had called for their carriage directly after Bea's dance with the duke at the Sheffield ball; she hadn't wanted anyone to know that no gentleman had requested Bea's hand for the supper dance, meaning she would have to dine with the matrons. It would be better, Lady Alcon had decided, to plead a sudden headache and leave immediately.

Bea had spent a solid two hours in the afternoon assuring herself that Lady Regina was merely a woman, albeit an unpleasant one. One could ignore her. Walk away. Be courageous and not respond to niggling remarks. Not hide!

Even so, she followed Lady Alcon with her stomach in a knot. The assembly hall was a large room hung in pale blue draperies, with a balcony at one end. The people who clustered in such a balcony, in Bea's experience, did so to poke fun at those dancing below.

She felt ill at the very sight of it; the last time she'd danced beneath a balcony, a guest hooted a witticism about the longitude and the latitude meeting in one place. Since Bea had been dancing with a gentleman as tall and thin as a beanpole, she had no difficulty grasping that she represented the globe's mid-section.

No music was playing at the moment. Ladies in colorful gowns were clustered on the dance floor, gentlemen dotted amongst them like the black spots on the back of a ladybug.

With a sickening thump of her heart, Bea caught sight of the Duke of Lennox, which meant that his sister Regina was here. Her fingers tingled, as if blood had rushed from her head; she felt dizzy.

This is *absurd*. Ridiculous, cowardly, stupid … With each rebuke, her panic multiplied.

Query: The likelihood that Regina would be furious after Bea's "nearly graceful" dance with her brother?

Probability: 100%.

Regina had meant to shame her, given that all eyes watched when the Duke of Lennox—who rarely appeared in society—took the floor. Yet Lady Alcon thought the dance might have brought Bea into fashion. It had led to the unexpected voucher for Almack's.

Regina would be *livid*.

"There's His Grace," Lady Alcon hissed, pinching Bea's arm. "Not that he'll dance with you again, but it is interesting to see him here. Perhaps he decided to choose a wife. If only he hadn't been such a dilly-dallier and made the decision last Season!"

Right.

Because then Miss Leodoldina Cottons would have been shoved in his face, and perhaps Lady Alcon would have scored a duke for one of her charges. That would have made her the most highly prized chaperone in all London.

Bea winced at the thought of what this Season was going to do for her chaperone's reputation. She didn't care for Lady Alcon, but she felt sorry for her. It wasn't easy for a lady to support herself in the manner to which she had been accustomed when her husband was alive.

Bea's father was paying not just for the privilege of Lady Alcon's introductions; he had also bought her a new wardrobe from *modistes* of her choice, as part of the contract they signed.

Just now the Duke of Lennox was standing with his back to them. Bea steered her chaperone to the far end of the room, happy to find a large statue of a Roman lady in a toga that could offer shelter if need be.

A small voice reminded her that she had vowed not to hide, but those words quickly melted away. Regina was here. Likely, her best friend, Lady Martha Telton-Sacks was here as well.

"Oh! I see Mrs. de Lacy Evans," Lady Alcon exclaimed. "Come along, Beatrice. She's so kind. I can prevail upon her to make her son escort you onto the floor. I wonder why the Master of Ceremonies hasn't begun the dancing yet."

Query: Would Bea provide entertainment to the gentlemen and ladies on the balcony?

Probability: 100%.

Mr. de Lacy Evans was precisely the beansprout who previously modeled the longitude to her latitude. Someday he would be a baron, and his mother was quite powerful in society, but he was still a beanpole.

Lady Alcon towed her through clusters of people to Mrs. de Lacy Evans' side, where the ladies exchanged condolences about the fog's unpleasant effects on one's joints.

After a while, Lady Alcon remembered that Bea was standing to the side, having edged about so that she was hidden from most of the room. "Come forward," she snapped, yanking Bea's arm.

Mrs. de Lacy Evans was not an unkind woman. She wasn't as thin as Lady Alcon, and she had sympathetic eyes. Of course, she'd gained her weight having five children, which was respectable.

Bea dropped a curtsy. "Good evening, Mrs. de Lacy Evans."

"Good evening, dear," she said. "Robert is looking forward to dancing with you, of course, and he has a friend with him tonight as well. So that's two dances."

She didn't pretend that Bea would be asked by anyone else, which was rather refreshing. From the moment Regina had spied her—well, spied Bea's hips, bottom, bosom, and all the other body parts that Regina found repulsive—she'd managed to make Bea an invisible pariah. Young men didn't even seem to see her, and try as she might, Lady Alcon couldn't force them to ask her for a dance.

Bea summoned up a smile. "That's very kind of you."

"I think my son is developing an infatuation with you, my dear," the lady said, unexpectedly. "He asked me this morning if you would be here, or at that play everyone is attending."

"I had tickets to the opening night of *The Wedding Dress*," Lady Alcon said importantly. "I handed them off to a nephew." She lowered her voice. "I haven't had time to tell you, Mrs. de Lacy Evans, but thanks to the kindness of Lady Regina, Bea danced with the Duke of Lennox last night at Lady Sheffield's ball."

"The kindness of Lady Regina?" the lady repeated, a dubious look on her face.

Apparently, she was more perceptive than Lady Alcon. Bea's chaperone wasn't precisely unobservant; she simply held the aristocracy in such reverence that she couldn't imagine Regina being... well... Lady Regina.

"Oh, there you are!" Mrs. de Lacy Evans exclaimed, before Lady Alcon had time to assure her that Lady Regina was as kind as kind could be. "Robert, here is Miss Valentine."

Bea curtsied before Mrs. de Lacy Evans's tall son. Someday he would have shoulders to match his legs... perhaps. At the moment he was made even taller by a mop of curls. But he had his mother's eyes and a nice cleft in his chin.

Rather to her surprise, he scrawled his name in two places on her dance card. She whispered, "You needn't do that!"

"Do what?" he asked, handing back her card.

She used the little pencil hanging from a ribbon to cross off one. "You needn't dance with me more than once, Mr. de Lacy Evans. I think it's very kind of you to obey your mother as it is."

His brows drew together. "You're an odd girl, Miss Valentine."

"I'm trying to be honest," she said indignantly.

"If I'm honest, I am looking forward to dancing with you more than with any other lady here." He leaned forward, and those sweet eyes had a different expression in them, one that startled Bea. "In fact, I'd dance with you three times, if I was allowed."

Before Bea could answer, another man stepped forward. "Mrs. de Lacy Evans, wouldn't you introduce me to Miss Valentine?"

It was *him*.

Lord Peregrine.

"Miss Valentine, may I present Lord Peregrine," the lady said as calmly as if pigs flew by her windows all the time.

"I'm honored to meet you," Bea breathed, sinking into a curtsy before Regina's fiancé. The most handsome man in the room.

Actually, in all of London.

Not only that, but Lord Peregrine was the man whom she couldn't stop thinking about in inappropriate ways. Bea managed an uncertain smile as he plucked up her dance card and scrawled his name—on the supper dance!

"Won't you dance that with Lady Regina?" she asked, before thinking.

Lady Alcon tittered. "What a question, Beatrice! He wouldn't ask you unless he were free. I expect that dear Lady Regina asked him to accompany you. She is an extraordinarily kind girl. A leader in polite society at her age!"

"She did," Lord Peregrine confirmed, flashing Bea a look from his black eyes.

It wasn't exactly an admiring look.

Bea felt herself turning the precise color of claret.

Before she could respond, another man stepped forward, and Lord Peregrine gave ground, walking off without another word.

This man was her father's height, whicxh is to say, just right: his head only slightly taller than hers. He had a thick head of dark hair, sturdy shoulders, and eyes that twinkled with laughter.

Bea assumed that he was Robert de Lacy Evans's friend—the one whom his mother had mentioned—but it turned out that Lord Argyle didn't know Mr. de Lacy Evans at all. A bit after that, Mr. de Lacy Evans's aforementioned friend, Peter Caron, did show up, jostling his way into the crowd.

By then, Bea was cautiously enjoying herself.

Lord Argyle was good-naturedly elbowing Mr. Caron and trying to get hold of her dance card, while Mr. de Lacy Evans was still claiming he wanted to put down his name twice.

She found herself laughing at their silliness. It was like being at home in the local assemblies, where she knew all the fellows and liked them.

Back in Cheshire, boys regularly fell in love with her, only to be told by her father that Bea was destined for better than a farmer's son; she would be going to London for a Season.

She'd never thought of herself as distasteful until she came to London.

A fourth man miraculously joined the first three.

They stood around her like a forest of tall trees. Like a fence, really. No one could see her, and that made Bea feel like herself. She started laughing and talking to them the way she talked to the boys at home.

"You see," Lady Alcon hissed. "Lady Regina's kindness has paid off. We cannot thank her enough. You owe her everything, Beatrice!"

Chapter 6

Almack's Assembly Hall

Fiennes Lawrence Peregrine was bored.

It wasn't a new experience, but it seemed acutely painful this evening. He considered Almack's to be the most tedious dancehall in London and only attended on the request—or rather, the demand—of his fiancée. Wherever he looked in the ballroom, he found girls in pale dresses watching him with hungry eyes.

They weren't watching *him*: they saw Fiennes as an embodiment of his father's wealth, a hunk of gold bullion disguised as a man. He discovered he was scowling and forced himself to put on a bland expression. He just had to get through the next month, marry Lady Regina, and then he would be free.

Free? Ridiculous to say that about marriage, but it was a fact. In his life, his father had asked him for only one thing: that he marry into the nobility. Fiennes didn't like Regina overly much, but that didn't matter. His own parents rarely spent time together, which likely explained his lack of siblings.

Fiennes strolled through eddies of gentlefolk, wondering vaguely why he didn't see his fiancée anywhere. Regina had insisted that he meet her at Almack's, and moreover, had ordered him to ask her friend for the supper dance.

He had complied, though it occurred to him now that he'd better make it clear to Regina that he wouldn't attend lackluster events like this in the future.

It wasn't until he was bowing before Miss Valentine as the supper dance began that Fiennes had thought to question Regina's command.

He was used to blushing debutantes, but Beatrice Valentine wasn't his fiancée's usual cup of tea. Regina's friends were scrawny, pert girls with glistening smiles and avid eyes.

To a one, they'd managed to insinuate that if he broke his engagement to their close friend, they would be happy to fill in. That included the curly-haired lady betrothed to an earl, which just went to show that money trumped blood these days.

But Miss Valentine?

After an initial blush, they met and parted in the steps of a quadrille, and she made absolutely no effort to enchant him. Not that it bothered him. He went back to thinking about an article in *The London Times* referencing England's massive public debt, until her silence made him remember the generally ignored rule that a gentleman must initiate conversation during a dance.

"How is your experience of London?" he asked. He was pretty sure she was from Cheshire, given her soft accent.

"Incomparable," his dance partner replied.

That was irony in her voice. Fiennes looked at Beatrice Valentine more closely. She had a clear-eyed pragmatism that he rarely saw in young ladies.

"What were you thinking about earlier, Lord Peregrine?" Miss Valentine asked. "You appeared to be deep in thought."

He answered honestly. "England's war debt."

"It's far too large, isn't it? My father is quite concerned."

Fiennes blinked at that.

She gave him a slight smile. "My father owns a country bank. He doesn't trust the new high-yield bonds."

"Interesting," Fiennes replied. "Neither do I. Nor do I trust the wartime bond issues."

"Too much easy credit," Miss Valentine said, nodding. "The Bullion Report didn't help."

They parted again, processing forward and back.

"Once again, I agree," Fiennes said when they were back on the sidelines. "What does your father think about the suspension of the gold standard?"

"He is concerned about government debt." Miss Valentine hesitated. "He is more optimistic, but I think that we'll be lucky to get through the next decade without a bail-out from a foreign bank."

He frowned.

"An infusion of gold reserves, say from the Banque de France," she added.

They separated for a few steps before Miss Valentine returned to his arms. He twirled her about, pleased that the music was drawing to a close. It would be interesting to eat a meal with her.

"What do you and your father feel about speculative ventures in America?" Fiennes asked, as they waited to enter the dining room.

"My father is enamored. I don't believe they are a good idea." Miss Valentine replied, adding, "I use the word 'enamored' with intent."

"Mr. Valentine appears to be both speculative and conservative," Fiennes noted, once they were seated. He couldn't see Regina anywhere. She had said they would eat together, so he chose a table for four.

A footman set down a selection of withered-looking ham sandwiches. "These are revolting," Fiennes observed, poking at them with a fork.

Miss Valentine gave him a wry smile. "It's my first visit to Almack's, but even I know that the food is reputed to be terrible."

"Has your father made extensive investments in America?" Fiennes asked. Her eyes were shining with intelligence.

"I have managed to curb his enthusiasm," she replied. "I believe a local bank, like ours in Cheshire, is best served by investing in local canals and mines. My father remembers when there were only five stocks available on the London Exchange, so he is thrilled by the ability to invest in foreign countries."

"My father is fond of talking of those days too," Fiennes said.

With a flutter of skirts, Lady Regina appeared at his left side. "There you are!" she cried, in a petulant voice that told him she was in a temper.

Fiennes rose. "Good evening, Lady Regina." He bowed and kissed his fiancée's hand. She was wearing the diamond he gave her over her white glove, which struck him as slightly gauche.

"Good evening, Lennox." He bowed before his fiancée's brother.

To his right, Miss Valentine was making her curtsies. Surely that wasn't despair in her eyes? She might be intimidated by Regina. His fiancée was at the very top of society, and the daughter of a country banker may well be overawed.

"Miss Valentine and I have been discussing the gold standard," he said, after they all sat down. Somewhat to his surprise, Miss Valentine didn't chime in; she was staring at her lap.

"I certainly hope that is an exaggeration," Regina said with a titter. "No true lady knows anything about coinage, and certainly not enough to *discuss* it! One can only describe such behavior as vulgar." She looked across the table. "Surely my dear Lord Peregrine was wrong, Miss Valentine. It's so *greedy* to discuss profits and investments. So unladylike."

"Look here—" Fiennes said.

But he was interrupted by the Duke of Lennox. "I don't see why ladies should pretend to ignorance of money, Regina. You were very interested in the details of your dowry. You and I went over the investments closely."

Regina's cheeks turned red, and she tossed her head like a recalcitrant horse. "That is scarcely the same thing! It is extraordinarily ill-bred to discuss the gold standard—whatever that is—whereas a dowry is a gift that accompanies the vow of sacred matrimony."

"Money is money," Fiennes pointed out.

"A lady never discusses mercantile commerce," Regina said, throwing Miss Valentine a spiteful look.

Luckily, the lady missed it, as she was still staring at her gloved hands.

The two women definitely weren't friends, which begged the question why Regina had directed him to bring Miss Valentine to supper. Presumably, she did so to poke fun at her. This was precisely why Fiennes disliked going about in society, and why he had nothing to do with ladies.

"I wouldn't expect you to understand, Lord Peregrine," Regina said, a sharp edge in her voice. "I certainly hope that *you* won't take up an avid pursuit of money. That wouldn't do."

Only one person in the world, his father, was allowed to command Fiennes. Even in that case, Fiennes only obeyed out of love and genuine respect. "Perhaps I misunderstand you, Lady Regina."

His fiancée gave him a narrow-eyed look. "I doubt that. I was straight-forward."

Miss Valentine cleared her throat. "I believe I shall make a visit to...if you'll excuse me." She began to rise.

The Duke of Lennox sprang to his feet. "I will escort you."

He left without so much as a backward look at his sister, taking Fiennes's supper partner with him. Fiennes waited until they were well away from the table before he sat down beside Regina once more.

"We'd better get one thing straight," he said. "I will never take orders from you as regards my daily activities, which certainly include an avid pursuit of money—an occupation that any sensible woman would encourage, by the way."

Regina's lower jaw fell open, which was not an attractive look. "How dare you!" she hissed.

Fiennes picked up one of the sandwiches and bit into it. The bread resisted his teeth, and the ham was so thinly sliced that he couldn't taste it. He swallowed and said, "I have no intention of emulating your father. Of spending lavishly and never making money."

"Gentlemen do not *make money*," Regina cried. "The very meaning of 'esquire' says as much. My father lived on the profits from the ducal estate, which are extensive."

"Those lands were ill-managed, depleted by careless replanting of wheat. I don't envy Lennox the task of bringing his fields back from insolvency. I'd be surprised if he harvests more than a few bushels."

The duke clearly had not shared that news with his sister. A pulse began to throb in Regina's forehead. "That is not my concern!" she snapped. "I am a *lady*, and as such, I should be safeguarded from such unpleasantries."

Fiennes picked up his lemonade, considered it, and placed the glass back onto the table. "I hope that we won't have to maintain an exhausting fiction about your delicate sensibilities once we're married, Regina."

She was a pretty girl, but he didn't like the hardness in her eyes and couldn't believe he hadn't seen it before.

"What could you possibly mean?" she inquired, a dangerous note in her voice.

Fiennes didn't give a damn about her temper.

"You can pretend to ladylike sensitivity in public, if you wish. You may not have noticed, but our dinner companions have deserted us as a direct result of your peevish response to a thought-provoking topic. I should hope we can discuss more than trivialities for the rest of our lives. I was interested to hear Miss Valentine's views on American investments."

"I don't even know where America is! You can't want me to be anything like Beatrice Valentine. You know why *she* talks about banking matters, don't you?"

"Because she has a sound intellect?"

"Because that's all she's got to offer," Regina snapped. "She's as swollen as a beet, so of course she brings up money whenever she can. She'll have to buy a husband using her father's coin as a lure."

Fiennes had had enough. "So did you, although in your case, your father did the work for you. He sheltered your dowry from the atrophy of the estate."

"I don't know what you're talking about!" she said shrilly. "I could have any man whom I wished."

She apparently caught a trace of derision in his expression. She leaned across the table and added with emphasis, "Any man I wanted in *all London.*"

Her bodice gaped, giving Fiennes a clear glimpse of not very much.

"That boast was not ladylike, Regina," he said, not bothering to hide his amusement. "Are you expecting me to fall about with gratitude at being the chosen one?"

Regina drew in a sharp breath. "You asked me to marry you!"

"Our fathers reached that agreement, as you know. Now I'm wondering whether I made a mistake in complying."

"You daren't say that to me!"

"You are attracting attention," Fiennes advised, feeling a pang of pity. The girl would never get a husband if society discovered her temper. His own mind was made up. He loved his father, but not enough for this.

"*You!*" Regina hissed.

He raised an eyebrow.

"I wouldn't marry you if you were—"

"The last man on earth?" Fiennes finished her cliché since anger seemed to have stifled her voice.

"I'll marry someone much better than you!"

"I don't doubt it. Why don't you keep the ring?" Hopefully, his voice wasn't too cheerful. Of course, now he'd have to find another noblewoman, a prospect that made his heart sink. Just look at Miss Valentine; a banker's daughter would make a better spouse.

Regina began hauling at the diamond ring, trying to pull it over her bunched-up glove. "Take this back, you, you reprobate!" She managed to remove the diamond ring and fling it at him. It bounced on the table and landed in a glass of lemonade.

Regina burst out laughing, shrill notes that attracted attention from every table that wasn't already eagerly watching the spectacle. "I lowered myself to marry you," she cried. "*You*, whose father smells of the shop!"

Pure rage poured into Fiennes's veins. He wasn't easily angered, but his family was his soft spot. His father had sent him off to Eton at the age of seven, and scarcely allowed him to come home for fear that his son would be contaminated by the "smell of the shop," as Regina put it. But Fiennes loved him.

His muscles went rigid, outrage sinking into his bones. "My father is not a subject for casual conversation."

"I should say not!" Regina tossed her head again. "No one would wish to discuss your mother's disgrace, running away to marry a merchant! Your pedigree was a concern when I agreed to marry you, and I should not have overlooked it."

Fiennes gave her a deliberately insolent smile. "Your temper would have been a concern, had I known you better."

She leaned forward over the table, her eyes livid. "I warn you, Lord Peregrine."

He shot her an incredulous glance. "Warn me of what?"

"I shall ruin you," Regina hissed. "You'll have to settle for a grocer's offspring, the way your mother did."

He burst out laughing.

In one swift movement, he upended the glass of lemonade on the wilted sandwiches, plucked up his diamond, and dried it with his napkin.

He stuck the ring in his pocket, knowing that every eye in the room was on him.

Then he moved back a step and bowed. "Good evening, Lady Regina."

Chapter 7

Miss Valentine—or Beatrice, as he thought of her—had indicated a wish to visit the ladies' retiring room, so Jonah escorted her out of the dining room. "If you could be anywhere in the world right now, where would you like to be?" he asked, as they walked.

It was a foolish question, not the sort of thing one asked a young lady.

"In the barn on my father's estate," Beatrice replied immediately.

A surprising answer. "Why?"

"The barn isn't clean, exactly, but it isn't dirty the way London is." She wrinkled her nose. An adorable nose, he noticed. "London streets smell of coal and smoke."

"True."

"The barn has a peaceful smell that comes from old leather and tired horses. With the peppery scent of lineament."

"If your father's barn is like mine, there's a whiff of the ale the stable hands drink secretly in the tack room."

"Better than something stronger, so my father says." She looked up at him, her eyes alight with amusement. "I thought you were a city creature, Your Grace."

"I'm only in London for my sister's debut," Jonah said. "I haven't taken up my seat in the House of Lords because there's too much to do in the country. I usually spend the year at the duchy."

Her eyes asked a silent question.

"My father left our lands in poor shape." He couldn't imagine why he was telling her this; if an acquaintance dared to bring up the subject, he would snub him roundly.

They reached the door of the ladies' retiring room, but he managed to keep her with him by dint of spilling details about the estate's neglect and the work he was doing to repair fields exhausted by repeated wheat crops.

"Have you tried sowing clover, Your Grace?" Beatrice asked. Her eyes met his frankly, without a hint of coyness.

"Jonah," he said. "Please call me Jonah."

She frowned at him.

"I only shared the ill effects of my father's neglect with my friends. Ergo, you are a friend."

"Absolutely not," she said, without even pausing to think about it. "I suggest clover, because apparently it adds nutrients to the soil. And I recently read about an iron plow with interchangeable parts that might also help with aeration."

They were still talking when a lady who had passed them and gone into the retiring room came back out and gave them a sharp look. Beatrice bit her lip, and promptly curtsied. "Good evening, Your Grace."

Jonah wanted to catch her arm and keep her with him, but instead he bowed and walked back slowly to the dining room. No woman of rank had ever looked at him so directly and spoken to him so frankly, without giggles or suggestiveness.

Beatrice was polite but showed no signs of interest in him. Not even in being his friend.

It abruptly occurred to him that he wanted far more than friendship.

It wasn't a matter of her lush figure, or her beauty, or even her lower lip. She smelled like lemons and soap, not a sophisticated fragrance. Yet he only had to touch her hand to feel heat spreading down his body with reckless speed.

When he reached their table, he was greeted by his sister, sitting alone, an ominous light in her eyes.

"What happened to Lord Peregrine?" Jonah asked.

"I sent him away," she said acidly. "He is a miserable *rat* whom I will never marry."

Jonah sank into a chair next to Regina, all thoughts of Beatrice fleeing his mind. "You did what?"

"I gave that man back his ring," she snarled. "He suggested that I keep it! As if I would want that filthy diamond as a reminder of him!"

Jonah's heart sank. Their father had accepted a large sum of money a decade ago when he set up the betrothal. Now Jonah would have to repay the Peregrines.

Somehow.

"I wish to return home immediately," Regina stated. "Where's that stupid chaperone of mine?"

"Mrs. Hastings is dining with Lord Fencibles," Jonah said. He nodded at Mr. Paine, the Master of Ceremonies, who was hovering not far away. Paine bowed, managing to convey without words the fact that the ducal carriage had already been summoned.

"This never would have happened if it hadn't been for that utter cow, Beatrice Valentine!" Regina spat. Her cheeks showed flags of anger.

Jonah had been on the verge of offering to escort Mrs. Hastings and Regina home, but the impulse died. "Your insult is untrue and unkind, Regina."

"Don't tell me you're going to start giving *me* lessons in comportment!"

Her voice had a dangerous ring that brought to mind hysterical tantrums Jonah remembered from her childhood. He made a stab at a more conciliatory remark. "It seems you and Lord Peregrine are not well suited."

Regina let out a derisive laugh. "You're saying that now? You told me it was an excellent match."

Four matrons at a nearby table were watching them intently. "It *was* an excellent match," Jonah said in a low voice. "Our father set it up a decade ago for that reason."

The late duke had desperately needed money, but as far as Jonah knew, Regina didn't know that detail.

She scowled at him. "Peregrine is a lowborn pig. Despicable. He insulted me after you left the table."

Jonah stiffened. He didn't know Lord Peregrine well—he had gone to Harrow and Cambridge, whereas Jonah went to Eton and Oxford— but he had thought he was a decent fellow. "Insulted you how?"

"Oh, not like that. You needn't call him out. He ... he said things."

"That suggests he would have been an uncomfortable spouse," Jonah pointed out.

Regina knit her brow. "If I leave, and they all gossip about me, is it a sign of cowardice? Should I stay or go?"

"*You* spurned *him*, not the other way around," Jonah pointed out. "I will remain, making it clear that the broken betrothal was your choice. I'm certain Lord Peregrine will confirm that account."

"I was too quick to accept his hand," Regina said, smoothing the wrinkles on her gloved finger where her engagement ring used to sit. "That diamond was tiresomely ostentatious, didn't you think? What's more, I told him to take Beatrice Valentine to supper, and he did!"

Jonah just looked at her.

She curled her lip. "My next fiancé will be a man who won't obey me if I ask him to do something revolting."

A wave of anger hit Jonah. His sister's face looked positively foxlike, he noted, struck again by the conviction that he and his sister had nothing in common. "Miss Valentine is *not* revolting," he stated.

"Yes, she is. When she blushes, she looks as round and red as a radish."

Jonah gave Regina a look so biting that she started blinking, "Be careful, Sister. You will expose yourself to censure if your malicious remarks are overheard. I will escort you to the carriage." He rose.

His sister's chaperone, Mrs. Hastings, deserted her dinner companion and bustled over. "You poor dear," she said to Regina. "I assure you that everyone is in full sympathy. How dare he?"

"Full sympathy? How dare he *what*?" Regina's voice had a dangerous chill to it.

Mrs. Hastings fell back a step. "Well, he … that is … Lord Peregrine … "

"I'm sure Lord Peregrine was unsettled by being jilted," Jonah said. "You'll leave me to deal with him, Regina. Any complaints will make him look the fool, and I will tell him as much."

"He was lucky that I even considered him," his sister said moodily.

Behind Regina's shoulder, Mrs. Hastings threw Jonah a troubled look; whatever Peregrine had done, he hadn't aired his sorrow at being jilted.

"Tomorrow is the ball in honor of Cecilia Paget's debut," Mrs. Hastings said in a determinedly cheerful tone. "Lady Paget has already assured me that she will consider you a guest of honor alongside her daughter."

"I shall escort you both to the carriage," Jonah said, drawing his sister to her feet. He was rather proud to see Regina walk through the dining room, smiling and nodding at acquaintances as if nothing had happened.

If nothing else, his sister had backbone.

Bea was dancing one of those quadrilles that involved endless prancing forward and backward, while trying to overhear enough gossip to understand what had happened between Lord Peregrine and his fiancée.

She had remained in the ladies' retiring room until her chaperone found her. The dinner hour was over, and dancing had begun again.

Clearly, *something* had happened. She and Lady Alcon had only just walked into the dancing hall when Lord Peregrine sauntered up to her with a wicked glint in his eye, kissed her hand, and thanked her for the supper they didn't even share. She hadn't time to respond before he walked away, loudly informing a friend that she was "exquisite."

All of this within earshot of Lady Martha Telton-Sacks, one of Regina's closest friends.

Bea wasn't stupid enough to think he had offered her a real compliment. Lord Peregrine had been mildly interested in talking about the gold standard, but he wasn't attracted to her.

On the other hand, he had obviously grasped that his fiancée disliked her, which meant that she was trapped in a fight between Regina and Lord Peregrine.

Could it be true that they had broken their engagement?

Suddenly she realized that Lord Argyle was trying to talk to her during the snippets of dance when they stood beside each other. *Had been* trying to talk to her, in fact.

"Is something wrong, Miss Valentine?" he asked now.

Lord Argyle had sunny blue eyes. He was as sweet as a milk calf, Bea thought absently. "Not at all," she said, so grateful that Regina didn't seem to be on the dance floor that she gave him a lavish smile.

"I always have to mind my steps as well," he said, with a sympathetic wrinkle of his nose.

Argyle and she kept chatting every time they found themselves back at the sidelines, waiting as another couple paraded forward and back. After a while, Bea relaxed. Every time she looked around, Regina was nowhere to be seen. Perhaps she had returned home?

In her search for Regina, Bea noticed one very interesting thing: The Duke of Lennox had *not* returned home.

He was leaning against a wall off to the side, and although people kept coming up and talking to him, he didn't seem to do much talking. In fact, she caught him watching her several times. It was too ridiculous to even contemplate, but it felt as if—

Query: What was the likelihood that the Duke of Lennox fancied Miss Beatrice Valentine?

Prediction: Wholly impossible. 0%. And yet...

Their eyes met again.

He didn't have Lord Peregrine's chiseled features: even though he was an aristocrat at the very top of society, his chin was stubborn, his nose Roman, his cheekbones hewn rather than carved.

None of that mattered. Just standing there, he radiated confidence, a cool self-assurance that was probably bred into him.

She returned her gaze to Lord Argyle's cheerful face. He had four brothers and sisters. He loved the country and was interested in time-pieces and canals.

"I shan't get to dance with you again until tomorrow," he said in a complaining tone. "You are coming to Lady Paget's ball?"

She nodded.

"Save me the first waltz?"

She gave him a smile. "Of course!"

When Jonah returned to the dance floor after seeing Regina and her chaperone into the carriage, Beatrice was processing about with Robert Argyle.

Jonah looked around for Lord Peregrine, but he caught sight of Beatrice's rounded hips and fine ankles instead. She was a study in contrasts: her neck had a delicate curve, but her bosom was lush. Dark honey hair curled around her ears. He thought it might be long when it was down, perhaps long enough to reach her arse.

He wanted her.

The raw, bald thought shocked him even as certainty took hold of his mind.

Argyle wouldn't be a bad match for her; he would be a marquess in a few decades The man's eyes were warm as he looked at his dance partner. Abruptly Jonah was aware that tension was building in his muscles, so he turned and walked to the far side of the room.

Devin had flirted throughout supper with a merry widow. "Do you still wish to continue to the Pantheon?" Jonah asked, walking up to his friend, who had relinquished the lady to a dance partner.

Clearly Devin had already heard about Regina's broken betrothal. "Has your sister returned home?"

Jonah nodded. "I suppose I should talk to Lord Peregrine."

"I'd let it die. It wasn't the most gentlemanly behavior, but no one likes to see their ring thrown into a glass of lemonade."

"What did he do?"

"Declared within hearing of Lady Martha Telton-Sacks that if his father hadn't demanded he marry a noblewoman, he'd be courting Beatrice Valentine—whom I gather your sister acutely dislikes, or that's what Lady Martha reported, tittering all the time. I had the distinct impression that if Martha hadn't been both betrothed *and* your sister's dear friend, she would view the broken engagement as an opportunity to annex the Peregrine fortune."

Jonah held back a groan.

"I have promised one dance before we leave," Devin said.

Jonah grunted, not really listening. He caught sight of Beatrice again, laughing up at Argyle. Her luscious mouth was over-sized, he'd decided. Too big for her face.

"You can just prop up the wall, where you've been most of the evening," Devin was saying. "I'll find Miss Valentine when this—"

Jonah's hand shot out and caught his friend's arm. "You are not dancing with her."

Devin's brows drew together. "I signed her card for the second dance after supper, which is next, and so yes, I am."

That was unacceptable. "No." Jonah heard the growl in his voice.

"Christ Almighty," Devin said. "Just because of what Peregrine said? Your sister has already left. Even if she hadn't, Regina cannot insist that your friends ignore Miss Valentine."

"It isn't that." Jonah didn't say anything else because … what could he say? He didn't mean to take a wife. He had to get his estate back on solid ground before he even thought of such a thing. Matters had improved in the two years since his father's death, but the income was hardly where it needed to be to properly support a wife and family.

Yet Devin was dissolute and wild. A rake. Jonah would knock him out before he allowed him to dance with Beatrice.

"I may be losing my mind," he allowed. "I'd like to leave, if you please."

"How much have you had to drink?"

"There's nothing *to* drink," Jonah pointed out. "This is Almack's, in case you forgot."

"You might have been carrying a flask."

Jonah shook his head. He was sober.

Sober as a judge and yet mad as a hatter.

Devin muttered curses under his breath as they left the assembly hall. "Give Miss Valentine my apologies," he said to Mr. Paine.

The Master of Ceremonies bowed.

In the carriage, Devin squared his shoulders. "You and I have been friends for decades. But you don't want me to be anywhere near your sister. Now you won't even let me dance with Miss Valentine, a woman who's no relation to you, as far as I know."

Jonah ground his teeth. "You're my closest friend." A wry smile curled his lips. "I don't suppose you'd care to marry Regina? She's free."

"Damn you, no," Devin said, without heat. "I don't want to marry either of them. I don't want you treating me like a pariah, either."

"I apologize. Dance with whomever you wish."

"I'm in no mood for chaste ladies," Devin said with a wolfish grin. "Remember I was telling you about the current show at the Pantheon? Russian opera dancers dressed like daisies missing petals? Time to make a daisy chain."

He settled back happily, but Jonah was grumpily aware that he had no interest in plucking petals from a Russian dancer.

Damn it. He really had lost his mind.

Chapter 8

April 16, 1814
Lord and Lady Paget's ball in honor of their daughter Cecilia's introduction to society
Paget House, Soho Square

Bea dressed for the Paget ball with a knot in her stomach. She hadn't slept the night before, worrying over the fact that she had somehow become a bone of contention between Regina and her former fiancé, Lord Peregrine.

Even thinking of how enraged Regina must be made her feel pale and faint.

Before moving to London, she would have described herself as independent and courageous. She had been looking forward to finding a perfect man to marry.

Now she was praying for the end of the Season, or even better, a broken leg that would give her a decent reason to go home early. Yet only a little girl, a coward, would run home to daddy. He would be so disappointed.

In contrast to Bea's state of mind, Lady Alcon was in a better mood than she'd been for weeks. Invitations had poured into the house that morning, and when her chaperone wasn't cooing over them, she was applauding Lady Regina's benevolence.

Her usual irritability resurfaced when Bea made her way down the stairs. "What are you wearing? What *are* you wearing?"

Bea raised her chin. "A new gown." It hadn't been made by a London *modiste*, but she felt confident in it. Confidence mattered when a woman was walking onto a battlefield.

Lady Alcon's lip curled in disgust. "Salmon-colored satin?" she asked shrilly. "Are those bullion tassels?" She came over and plucked at them. "Hanging in *streamers* on one side? I've never seen anything like it. This is not a masquerade ball, you know. That bodice is low, given the over-abundance of your … abundance."

The fashion was to be slender as a reed and wear flowing, light gowns that billowed in the wind. Bea's body was soft and pillowy. In fact, her body filled in the shape that ladies' dresses made in a breeze.

"I like this gown," Bea stated. It wasn't salmon-colored. The petti-coat was rose and the bodice silver, edged with a superb border of blonde lace. It had been made by a French *émigré*, and in Bea's opinion, the wide lace border at the hem and the tassels would make it one of the most fashionable garments on the ballroom floor.

"How are your sleeves drawn in?" Lady Alcon inquired, coming closer.

"With embossed silver ornaments," Bea said, pointing them out. "It gives them a graceful puff."

"Humph," her chaperone grumbled, stepping back. "I will say that the lace is well accented by that diamond necklace and ear-rings."

"Lord Argyle asked for my first waltz," Bea told her, hoping to lead Lady Alcon toward happier thoughts.

"We'll be lucky if any other gentleman approaches you, given all that silver cord swaying at your side," she bit, but her sour tone didn't have the same ferocity behind it as it would have a week ago.

Bea thought that Lady Alcon was growing cautiously optimistic that Bea would be able to wrangle a husband by the end of the Season.

"No eating tonight," her chaperone ordered, temper roaring back. She was firmly of the opinion that lack of will was directly linked to weight. Sadly, the curves Bea had rather liked back in Cheshire were interpreted as the sign of an out-of-control appetite in London.

"I won't," Bea promised.

As soon as they entered Paget House, Lord Argyle bounced up to them and swept Bea into a waltz before she had a chance to locate Regina. That made her nervous: dancing was how Regina had first discovered her. Since that time, Regina had managed to bump into or kick Bea several times on the dance floor.

Once Regina had even tried to trip her up, though she apologized so prettily for wrapping her foot around Bea's ankle that Bea ended up looking like a lumbering cow, getting in the way of a graceful sprite.

They waltzed to one end of the ballroom and back without seeing Regina, so Bea relaxed enough to chat with Lord Argyle about the timepieces he loved so much. When the dance ended, she ought to have returned to her chaperone, but instead she remained with Lord Argyle. He was so comfortingly bulky that she felt sheltered and safe, and his enthusiasm for timepieces was adorable.

"We should make a timepiece that's as big as St. Paul's Cathedral, revolving on a great spire," he told her. "That way everyone in London would know what time of day it was at all times."

"Why?" Bea asked.

"Why? What do you mean *why*? If you know what time it is, you don't waste it!"

"I like wasting time," Bea said, grinning at him. "One could say that we're wasting time at this very moment."

"No," he said, shaking his head, even though he was smiling too. "Time with you would never be wasted, Miss Valentine. In fact, if you would be kind enough to give me the supper dance, we might join my mother and father, who are here tonight."

Well.

It seemed some gentlemen didn't think that Bea was too disgusting to marry anyone but a butcher.

"Certainly. Would you please escort me to Lady Alcon?" she asked. She had a strong feeling that her eyes were shining.

"Now that's a waste of time," he said, mock-grumpily.

They were making their way around the edge of the ballroom when she realized Regina, Martha, Prudence, and Petunia were strolling toward them, Martha's and Regina's arms wreathed around each other. As their eyes met, Regina's smile widened, and she waved.

Bea's heart began thumping in her ears.

"Friends of yours ahead," Lord Argyle said. "Would you like to greet them? I should find my partner for the next dance. I am looking forward to supper."

"As am I," Bea said, gulping. "I think I'd better ... Excuse me."

With that she dashed away, intent on putting as many bodies as possible between herself and Regina.

Bea could have given lessons in the Art of Survival to all the wall-flowers who would follow her into this miserable farce called the marriage market. More precisely, she could teach the skill of fleeing to the ladies' retiring room at any and all opportunities. Hiding was her forté.

Week One would cover the locations of ladies' retiring rooms, their size, how to reach them quickly in an emergency, and what kinds of errands would lead the attending maid to vacate the room for at least twenty minutes so that tears could be shed in private. She might offer a side-lesson in Avoiding Tears.

Week Two would teach the art of delicately, yet thoroughly, ripping one's own hem. A ruffle parted from a gown easily if threads had been loosened by its owner in the carriage. A significant rip might allow one to cozily hide away for as long as an hour while a maid stitched your gown back together.

Week Three would address the cheerful, evasive conversation necessitated by the arrival in the retiring room of ladies whose bodices had been torn by male hands, or who were dashing for a chamber pot. This week would also address female complaints of all kinds.

Bea was so caught up in her instructional plans—the attending maid having escorted a nauseated lady away a good ten minutes ago—that she didn't immediately react when the door to the retiring room opened.

By the time she raised her head, they were already in the room.

Clustering around her.

Heart racing, Bea jumped to her feet. The four of them stood in a semi-circle before her, shoulder to shoulder. She couldn't flee.

"Tubby Bea," Lady Regina said, baring her shining teeth. "I knew you'd be in here. Having a little meal, are you? Too hungry to wait until supper is called?"

"Lady Regina," Bea said, bobbing a curtsy. She forced herself to keep her chin up and meet each of their eyes. "Miss Prudence, Lady Martha, Miss Petunia."

"Martha should have been acknowledged before Prudence," Regina said with a shrill laugh. "You really mustn't act like such a boor. In more ways than one, obviously."

"Bovine is the word you're looking for," Martha said pleasantly.

You'd think Bea would be used to it by now, but somehow, she wasn't. Her heart threatened to pound itself out of her chest. "You're so humorous," she murmured, and took a step forward.

The girls didn't budge. It was amazing how impenetrable they were, given that their bodies were no more solid than willow boughs wrapped in gauze.

"Ew, crumbs," Prudence said, rubbing her toe on the carpet. "I suppose you concealed cake under that gunnysack you're wearing and then snuck off to gobble it in private."

Bea took a breath. She hadn't dared to eat anything outside her house since the first week of the Season, since the moment this group of girls chose her as their... their plaything. Their target.

Just at the moment, she was in the grip of such a vivid sense of dread that it was all she could do to stay on her feet.

She backed away until she reached the wall. The solid feeling of it was comforting, because she was still missing a hank of hair in the back, lost to a "slip of the fingers" after Prudence Massinger pulled a pair of embroidery scissors from her reticule.

"I won't keep you," Bea said, hating the sound of her own voice. She sounded so—so pitiful. Weak.

"*I* think you should get down on your hands and knees and pick up all those crumbs," Regina said.

"There are no crumbs," Bea said, keeping her eyes on Regina's face. She had learned that lesson. Regina might say the most appalling things, but she wouldn't elbow her "accidentally" if Bea was looking directly at her.

"Yes, there are!" Prudence said. "Don't tell me that you're short-sighted as well as fat."

At first, she didn't understand what was hitting her face, but a second later she realized that she was being pelted with crumbs of pastry, which weren't hard or hurtful, but that stung all the same.

Prudence was taking the time to aim each crumb. "I'm going for your cheeks," she said, when Bea looked at her. "God knows they're as big as moons, so it's not hard to hit my target."

"It's so kind of you to bring Beatrice some food," Regina cooed. She narrowed her eyes at Bea. "Of course, you'll have to clean up the mess on the floor before Lady Paget's maid returns."

"No," Bea managed. She turned her head to meet Regina's hard eyes, ignoring the hailstorm of cake. She'd heard that Arctic ice was gray. There couldn't be anything colder than Regina's eyes.

"Did you say 'no' to me?" Regina said softly.

Bea scarcely dared to breathe, but she forced words past her stiff lips. "I didn't bring food in here. Lady Prudence did."

"You're not suggesting that Prudence should get down on her knees and clean up? Just look at her. She's not a plough horse, the way you are. She's a *lady*."

"We can leave the cake for the maid," Bea whispered, feeling a foggy blanket of hopelessness descending around her shoulders.

"You think *she* should clean up this disgusting mess? I pity the maids in your house, I really do. If there are maids in your house."

That was unfair. It was all unfair. Bea found a retort trembling on her lips. Her father was a banker. She had a dowry—and unless she was mistaken, it was larger than Prudence and Petunia's dowries put together—but that didn't matter.

"You need exercise," Regina said. "Anyone can tell that. You should get down on your hands and knees, just the way a scullery maid does." Her eyes lingered on Bea's hips.

Bea drew in an unsteady breath and surprised herself.

"I won't."

Chapter 9

Bea was trapped, as when an enemy army surrounds a lone soldier. She swallowed hard. The soldier might die, but he could do so with dignity.

Regina took a step toward her, her hands going toward Bea's shoulders, planning to shove her down to her knees, apparently.

Bea braced her legs and pushed her shoulders against the wall. She loved to ride and could do so for hours. She loved to walk over the hills too, until she was hot and sweaty. Regina couldn't possibly be strong enough to push her down.

A flicker in the girl's eyes showed she had come to the same conclusion.

Easing back, Regina broke into a titter of laughter. "We ought to be sympathetic, because God knows all that flesh must need tending." The other girls obediently tittered.

Where was the maid assigned to the retiring room? After spending the last ten minutes in blissful silence, grateful for her absence, Bea found herself feverishly praying that the woman would reappear.

More than fifty ladies had been invited to the Paget ball. Didn't someone need to use the chamber pot discreetly tucked behind a screen?

She knew from experience that the moment the door opened, the girls would turn into a flock of sweet debutantes, as charming and kind as anyone could wish.

But now?

Martha snatched up Bea's reticule and turned it upside down. Bea had learned that lesson in the early days of the Season; there was nothing inside. Everything she might need was pinned to her chemise.

"I suppose you already ate," Martha sniffed. "You've been in here long enough to gobble a whole turkey."

"If you'll excuse me, I must return to the ballroom," Bea said. "My chaperone will be—"

"Oh, no, she won't," Regina said, smiling at her.

Bea's stomach lurched. That was Regina's worst smile. The one that looked eerily cold and slightly mad. "Why won't she?"

"Lady Alcon wasn't feeling well, the poor old dear. It hasn't been easy for her, chaperoning *you*. She's used to better fare. She confided to me that she feels humiliated. After all, two years ago she chaperoned Totty Balkin. *You* wouldn't know this, but Totty married an earl."

Bea did know that. Her chaperone was very fond of listing the favorable marriages she'd arranged before the mistake of taking on a fat country girl like Bea—one whose own mother would have despaired at the challenge of marrying her off, according to Lady Alcon.

Bea had been just a girl when her mother died, but she remembered her very clearly. She had been a famous beauty. It was awful to imagine her mother giving her a pitying or condemning look. Perhaps she would have suggested vinegar diets, the way Lady Alcon did, or dosed Bea with patent medicines guaranteed to melt away at least a stone in weight.

Or maybe she would have loved Bea the way she was.

"Are you telling me that Lady Alcon has returned home?" Given the fear clawing at her stomach, Bea was quite proud that her voice didn't shake. Her chaperone couldn't have left her alone. That was...that was illegal or something.

"I informed her that we would find a place for you in our carriage," Regina said, her smile saying without words that Bea could walk all the way to Cheshire before Regina gave her a seat. "I do believe that Lady Alcon has delusions that my brother might show you some interest, after the exhibit you made of yourself dancing with him."

The girls all laughed at that idea.

Bea pressed her lips together hard. She would not give Regina the satisfaction of seeing her cry. She could take a hackney home. She had a pound note pinned to her chemise.

"I promised Lady Alcon that you could sit beside him in the carriage...unless you'd prefer to go home with my former fiancé, Lord Peregrine? You could always beg *him* for a ride."

A curious silence fell over the room. Bea had the idea that Regina's friends were not certain what to say about the broken engagement. "I have no interest in Lord Peregrine or the Duke of Lennox," she stated.

"I suppose you didn't realize that Lady Alcon was feeling faint." Regina looked around. "You don't care about the mess that you're leaving for the maid. You really don't care about those that serve you, do you?"

Of course, she did. She *did*.

"Lady Alcon does not serve me," Bea said, straightening her back. She always used to stand straight. It was only after she moved to London for the Season that her backbone had grown a curve. Turned into taffy.

She looked at Prudence. "You spilled those crumbs. No, you *threw* food at me, as if I were a duck on a pond."

"I'd describe it as throwing food *to* you," Regina said brightly. "Prue was showing you a kindness."

Out of nowhere a flame of courage raced down Bea's body. "Why are you so interested in my appetite?" she demanded, her voice shaking. "You've been jeering at me since the day we met. Why? What did I do to you that you care about me or my hips?"

Regina scoffed, so Bea looked to her retinue: to Martha, whose eyes were expressionless; to Prudence, who looked—perhaps—faintly apologetic; and to Prudence's twin sister, Petunia, who was blinking confusedly. Petunia wasn't very bright, but she was so pretty that it didn't matter.

"You chose me at that very first ball of the Season," Bea said, looking back over them slowly. They were the four most beautiful girls on the market—*diamonds of the first water*—or so everyone said. "Why? It wasn't my fault that I bumped into Regina on the dance floor. My partner was visibly inebriated."

"We know when someone doesn't belong among us," Regina said sharply, her upper lip curling. She wasn't as beautiful when she did that.

"Why not just leave me be?" Bea said, making her voice as forceful as she could.

Regina tossed her head. "Tell her, Martha."

"We are in charge of society," Martha said, her soft voice hiding a nature that seemed as hard as rock. "My mother is one of the patrons of Almack's. We all know she made a mistake admitting you, but she didn't realize that you'd try to steal Regina's fiancé!"

"What are you talking about?" Bea burst out. "You're sixteen years old. Who made you the guardians of society? Why would you even care whether I'm at Almack's or not? I had nothing to do with Lady Regina's broken engagement. I'm not likely to steal any man you'd like to marry."

They all burst into laughter again. The sound rolled around Bea's head like the sound of children at play. Cruel children. The kind that torment kittens.

"*You?* Steal someone whom *we'd* consider marrying?" Regina could scarcely shape the words through her choking hilarity. "You can try! Well, you have tried, haven't you?"

Martha was laughing the hardest. "That's cracked!" she said gaily. "Everyone was amused at the way you looked at the Duke of Lennox as if you fancied him. As if you thought he might fancy you!"

"You really are a dunce," Prudence taunted.

"I plan to marry the duke," Petunia declared, "unless Prudence decides she'd rather have him, of course."

"I must be a dunce," Bea retorted, "because I don't understand why you are so cruel, the four of you. You're all beautiful. But you are not—"

Regina's hand flashed out, and Bea's head slammed back against the wall. Stunned, Bea raised a hand to her cheekbone. "Did you strike me?"

"Do you want to know why we've decided to cut you from the herd?" Regina demanded. "It's not because you're so fat, though God knows, that's disgusting enough."

"I'm leaving this room," Bea said. She looked to her left. Petunia was chewing her lip; Bea had the feeling that Regina had just surprised her. Without pausing, she dove between Prudence and Petunia.

"It's because you're a *slut*," Regina said, whipping about and jumping in front of the door, the only way out of the room. "You're nothing more than a great whore, and we all know it. That's why Peregrine said what he said about you."

"You're mad," Bea said. "You're as cracked as an old jug." She looked at the other three. "You should be ashamed of yourselves, following her. Listening to her."

She edged forward, but there was no way to move past Regina, who was standing before the door, next to a small table holding a pitcher and basin of water, so that ladies could wash their hands after using the chamber pot.

Regina snorted. "Don't you realize that the arbiters of society have responsibility? Martha's mother doesn't allow bad blood through the doors of Almack's. She takes her duties very seriously. Why, sometimes the meetings determining who may have a voucher last for hours."

"I already have a voucher," Bea said woodenly. Her cheek was throbbing as if she had a toothache.

"A decision made before you tried to steal Regina's fiancé," Martha said, sounding very reasonable. "No brassy whores allowed."

"I am not a whore," Bea said. "I am *not*." This was ridiculous. Asserting that she wasn't a whore was like maintaining that she wasn't a bluebird.

Regina snorted. "With the way you walk? With that chest—and that bodice? You have all your wares on view, for sale!"

Bea didn't look down. Her breasts were the kind that people thought of when they talked about "heaving bosoms." Just now her breaths were shuddering, and that meant her breasts were trembling too.

"Everyone knows," Regina taunted.

"Knows *what*?"

"That you're hungry for it." Her voice dropped. "You might as well just admit it."

"You are mad," Bea repeated.

"I'll bet you dampen your petticoats," Regina continued, curling her lips again. "My chaperone told me that it's a common practice among women who are hungry for a man between their legs."

"Ew," Bea said. "You're mad, and your mind is as filthy as a sink. Get out of the way, Lady Regina. If you don't let me out, I am going to scream. Everyone will hear."

"Oh?" Regina laughed with what sounded like genuine amusement. "What will you say when someone bursts through the door?"

"I'll say that I encountered an insect," Bea said. "A creature that belongs under a rock!"

Regina's laughter cut off, and a streak of red showed up high in each cheek. "You dare," she hissed. "I am the daughter of a duke, and you are a *nothing*."

"I'd rather be a nobody than one of you." Bea had crossed some sort of threshold from which there was no going back. "I'm proud not to be you," she said steadily. She glanced at the other girls. "I'm proud that I'm not your friend, that I have never, in my life, been as cruel and petty as the four of you are. I never will be," she added fiercely.

"That's a mean thing to say," Petunia said, an astonished look on her face. "That's not nice."

Her twin elbowed her in the ribs. "Shut up."

Regina cast Petunia a scathing glance. "You're going to listen to a woman like that?" She turned to the table holding the pitcher of water.

"You wouldn't dare!" Bea cried.

"Why don't we just make sure that everyone knows what a slut you are? They already know that you duck into retiring rooms to dampen your petticoats."

Bea gasped. "I hide to get away from *you*."

"Poppycock." Regina dipped one hand in the jug and dashed water at Bea's skirt.

"You're out of your mind," Bea gasped.

They all looked down. Water clearly marked the pink overskirt.

"Oh my," Regina mocked. "People are going to think that you spilled your slop."

Chapter 10

"Shut up!" Bea snapped.

Without conscious volition, her hand flashed to the pitcher, scooped up a generous handful of water, and dashed it at Regina.

Who screamed.

"Oh my, look at that," Bea said. She didn't know what had overcome her, but suddenly she didn't feel cowed in the least. Not by these silly girls.

Regina was plucking at her white skirts, which didn't show spots, but clung to her legs. In fact, Bea decided that Regina's limbs resembled those of a stork, and her knees stuck out like the wheels on a cart.

Martha fell to her knees and began dabbing ineffectively at Regina's gown with a towel.

When Bea registered that she wasn't the one on her knees, a little smile curled the edges of her mouth.

"You dare," Regina squawked, sounding dumbfounded and infuriated at once. "*You*—you're smiling? At me?"

"You wanted someone to kneel before you," Bea said, with a gasp of laughter. "Martha will have to do."

Behind Regina's shoulder, the door began to open.

Regina didn't notice; an unholy light had lit in her eyes. She wrenched her skirts out of Martha's hands, grabbed the pitcher, and tossed the contents straight at Bea.

Bea yelped as a wave of cold water struck her midsection, sinking instantly through her gown and chemise. At the same moment, she met the astonished eyes of their hostess, Lady Paget, standing in the doorway.

In the blink of an eye, Regina turned from an infuriated Medusa to an injured damsel. She dropped the pitcher back on the table, turned on her heel, and threw herself at Lady Paget. "Beatrice Valentine destroyed my toilette, and now I daren't return to the ball," she wailed. "The Earl of Winchester has asked me for the supper dance!"

Bea was shivering; her skirts were drenched, water running into her slippers. Lady Paget looked her over, shaking her head.

"I can't even summon a governess," the lady said, sounding stunned. "What we need here is a *nanny*."

Regina's narrow shoulders were shaking with sobs.

"Lady Regina had to defend herself," Martha cried. She was back on her feet, though Bea noticed that a big splash of water marked her gown in just such a position to suggest that she'd had an accident while using a chamber pot.

Lady Paget raised an eyebrow. She had put her arms around Regina, but Bea thought her patting seemed perfunctory. To this point, all society had followed Regina's lead. But Lady Paget looked less easy to fool, perhaps because she'd raised several children and knew a nursery fight when she saw it.

"Lady Regina threw water at me, intending to make it appear that I had dampened my petticoats," Bea explained. "For her part, Lady Prudence threw cake on the floor so that people would think I had retired here in order to eat."

Her explanation ended in a shiver. Bea was so cold that her teeth were chattering. From where she stood, Bea couldn't see any tears on Regina's face, although she was blotting her eyes with a handkerchief.

Lady Paget sighed and put Regina away from her. "Pull yourself together, my dear. We all know how high passions can run during the Season, particularly for those in their first year. I'm sure you're sorry, aren't you, Lady Regina?"

"Oh, yes, of course," Regina whimpered. "I lost my head."

Bea would *never* apologize, which Lady Paget obviously guessed, since she said, "Lady Regina, you may return to the ballroom. You'll be in time for the supper dance. Lady Martha, you may also return, but I suggest you remain seated until your gown dries."

Martha glanced down at her front and let out a yelp.

"I couldn't go back to the dance," Regina said, catching her breath, as if from a fit of violent sobbing. "My gown is damp!" She turned and looked at herself in the glass.

Bea thought Regina's damp gown was extremely unflattering, but Regina clearly didn't agree. Her lips curled appreciatively as she surveyed the way her skirts clung to her lean thighs. "Perhaps it's not *so* terrible."

"You won't be the only one with dampened petticoats," Lady Paget said dryly. "I shall be certain to inform everyone that your appearance is the result of an accident. Lady Martha, Lady Regina, I will speak to you later."

Bea realized that Prudence and Petunia had snuck out of the room at some point. She wound her arms around her breasts as Regina—with one last, virulent glare at Bea—left with Martha.

"You're too wet for further dancing, my dear," Lady Paget said to Bea. "I will, of course, be happy to inform the gentlemen who have signed your dance card."

It seemed her hostess hadn't been informed of her unpopularity. "Lord Argyle was the only person who had asked so far," Bea confessed.

"I'm sorry that your evening has ended in such an abrupt fashion," the lady continued. "I saw you dancing with Argyle, and it was obvious to all that you have made an impression on him. I hope we can bring him to the point, but not tonight. I'll summon your chaperone."

"Unfortunately, Lady Alcon developed a headache and left," Bea said miserably.

Lady Paget frowned. "She deserted you? What arrangements did she make for your return home?"

"Lady Regina assured her I would have a seat in her carriage."

Lady Paget's eyebrow shot up. "Lady Regina is giving away seats in her brother's carriage without informing him? That's quite presumptuous."

Regina hadn't had the faintest intention of taking Bea home, but Bea kept her mouth shut.

"I shall inform the duke," Lady Paget decided. "I expect he'll direct the carriage to bring you home and return later for his sister and himself."

A maid walked in and stopped short, her mouth falling open as she looked at the water-sopped carpet.

"Water everywhere, cake on the floor," Lady Paget said. "It's as if a family of rats rampaged through the chamber. You'll need to clean it up before anyone sees it. Where have you been?"

The poor maid blinked, and then said, "Mrs. Thatcher felt nauseated, so I took her upstairs for a rest, but once she was there, she grew quite ill. Nellie escorted two other ladies to the same chamber, and both lost everything they'd eaten. I came to find you because Nellie thinks that there may be something wrong with the salmon patty."

Lady Paget visibly paled. "Has it been removed from the refreshments table?"

"Yes, my lady, but you remember that Cook had shaped it into a dolphin. Only the long nose is left. Everything else was eaten up."

Bea took one of the lengths of toweling stacked next to the now-empty pitcher and put it on a bench so that she wouldn't soak the seat. Then she picked up another and wound it around her shoulders before she sat down.

The door eased open, and a liveried footman announced, with his head turned rigidly to the side so he couldn't see into the room: "Begging your pardon, my lady, but the Prince of Wales has taken ill."

In the horrified silence that followed, he added, "His Majesty cast up his accounts on the billiards table, and Lord Paget thinks the felt will have to be replaced."

"Felt!" Lady Paget cried, wild-eyed. "Who cares about felt? The heir to the kingdom might die due to salmon prepared in *my* kitchens!"

"His Majesty had drunk a large tankard of whiskey as part of a bet, my lady. It's hard to know whether he ate the salmon, as he's quite inebriated and isn't capable of answering questions."

"His Majesty loathes fish paste," Bea put in.

From the way Lady Paget visibly jumped, she'd forgotten all about her. "He does? How do you know that?"

The Regent had caught Bea's attention at her third ball. By then, Regina and the others were already well into their torment of Bea, but she had held out hope that her form was distasteful only to the four of them.

Then she'd run into the Prince Regent in a dusky corridor. She had dropped a deep curtsy, straightening to find His Majesty looking her up and down, swaying slightly.

"You're a fine heifer," the prince had said. The words sank into Bea's ears like a blow. "Fat and frolicking, I've no doubt." He'd reached out as if he was going to pinch her.

She had turned around and fled, running as fast as she could. But it hadn't stopped her from hearing the Regent's irritated bellow. "A woman with kettledrums the size of yours should stay put!"

That night, she'd been so horrified at the idea that the Regent might make public comments about her "kettledrums" that she pretended a headache and went home. Since then, she'd watched the Regent as closely as she could, if only to avoid his attention.

"I doubt His Majesty ate the salmon," she told Lady Paget. "Last week I heard him tell Lord Marcellus that seafood is fattening."

"Thank goodness," the lady said, patting her heart. "A drunk monarch is nothing out of the ordinary, but a poisoned one would be disastrous." She turned to the footman. "Tell Radcliffe that I'll be along to take care of His Majesty as soon as I arrange for Miss Valentine to be taken home."

"I'll fetch a mop, my lady," the maid said, leaving after a last narrow-eyed look at the wet, food-strewn room.

"I'm so sorry," Bea said, waving at the floor. "I tried to leave as soon as I realized Lady Regina and her friends had entered, but it was difficult."

"Where is your father?" Lady Paget asked.

"He returned to Cheshire."

At first, they'd both been excited to come to London, certain Bea would quickly find a husband. Her father had been confident and generous, telling her that he would never accept an offer without consulting her first. He'd shared stories about the offers her mother had received, and the thrill, the exultation, he'd felt when she chose him over the others.

Needless to say, things had gone differently for Bea.

Her father had remained in London for two weeks, waiting for bouquets of posies, morning calls, invitations, all the things that were supposed to happen. He had to return to his bank after that; besides, they'd both surmised by then that suitors were unlikely to line up at the door.

Lady Paget was frowning. "I do not condone the practice of handing young ladies over to paid chaperones. Look at Lady Alcon's behavior. As if her failures of last Season weren't egregious enough, she left you at a ball without a suitable chaperone and scarcely a way to return home. I shall have a word with her about her lax behavior."

Bea could just imagine Lady Alcon's reaction to that.

Lady Paget opened the door. "Come along, dear. I'll bring you to the library. There's a warm fire, and you can dry off. It will take time for His Grace's carriage to be brought around. You certainly don't want to stay here and have to explain why you are wet!"

Query: What percentage of Lady Paget's guests would believe that the lovely Lady Regina had dashed a pitcher of water at her?

Probability: Perhaps... 1%.

She had the odd feeling that Regina's brother, the duke, might believe her.

Chapter 11

Jonah gave his sister's dance card a cursory glance. "You might want to avoid Freddy Arbuthnot. Word has it he's gambled away his entire allowance again."

"He'll be a marquess someday," Regina argued.

Jonah shrugged. "A penniless marquess would make an uncomfortable husband."

"He won't spend *my* money."

"Your money is in the form of a dowry," Jonah explained. "It will belong to him as soon as you marry."

Regina smiled. "No, it won't."

If any woman could overturn the English legal system, it would be Regina. He couldn't remember a single occasion in their childhood wherein she hadn't gotten her way.

"Gambling holds a powerful allure," he said, trying again. "I've seen Arbuthnot at the tables until three in the morning."

"Not if I decide to marry him," Regina stated.

He almost had sympathy for the gambler, but someone had to marry Regina. Having done his duty, he handed her to a young gentleman who vainly tried to hide his excitement at dancing with a duke's daughter.

"You have a problem," Devin said, appearing at his shoulder without warning.

"What?"

His friend gestured at Regina, who was briskly dragging the boy into the lead position in a country dance.

"Your sister."

"What about her?" Jonah turned and surveyed the ball room again. What had happened to Miss Valentine? Not that he planned to dance attention on her, but he thought he might take her in to supper. Since he was here.

"She's dampened her skirts," Devin said, in a lowered voice.

For a moment, Jonah thought he was talking about Beatrice Valentine. A dizzy, fleeting image of *that* young lady in wet skirts that clung to her curvy body lanced through his mind.

"Not only is it unsuitable," Devin continued, "but she'll gain a reputation as soon as the dowagers notice."

"Are you talking about Regina?" Jonah said, belatedly making sense of the conversation.

"Yes," Devin said impatiently. "Your sister. Your little sister. The one I warned would likely get into trouble without a mother, and she has. She's dampened her petticoats, Lennox. It must be a reaction to her broken engagement."

Jonah was aware of a stultifying don't-give-a-damn feel about Regina, but he suppressed it. "You must be mistaken. Regina is judgmental of ladies who try to attract attention in such a crass fashion."

That was an understatement. Regina's ability to spit venom was legendary in their extended family, but she went from critical to lacerating when a woman's virtue was at issue.

"Take a look," Devin said, nodding toward the ballroom. "Wait until she turns in our direction."

Once Regina turned, there was no mistaking the way her skirts clung to her legs. He remembered his sister's knees from when she was a small girl. It was disconcerting to realize that they still dominated her legs. "I suppose I should take her home," he said, scowling.

"No," Devin said. "As a man with four sisters, I can promise that it would only lead to a scene. In the carriage on the way home, say something brief and pointed. If you phrase it right, she'll appreciate the tip."

Jonah tried to imagine Regina expressing gratitude at advice from him but defaulted to the image of an angry tiger. Or a cobra.

Devin began jovially giving him advice on how one might interact with a normal sister, and he kept nodding at regular intervals out of pure politeness. What Devin didn't realize is while lust inspired by dampened petticoats could presumably drive a man to ungentlemanly behavior, that threat didn't apply in this case.

Enraptured by *those* kneecaps?

No.

Instead, the thought brought him back to Miss Valentine. If she were his sister—his soul-deep revulsion at that idea was shocking—and she'd dampened her petticoats, he'd have dragged her off the ballroom floor.

All the men would have been gaping at her thighs. That would be unacceptable. Entirely unacceptable. The thought made him feel twitchy, and he never felt twitchy.

Devin grimaced at him. "There's something off about you this evening. You've got a ... a pale-eyed stare, like a man on the point of death or something."

That startled Jonah. "My eyes are not pale!"

"You know what I mean." His friend peered closer. "You're not falling ill, are you?"

"I believe I might get married after all." He made the statement nonchalantly.

"You told me that you couldn't marry for at least two years, due to the condition of the ducal estate," Devin pointed out.

That was true. But it was even more true that if he didn't marry Bea, she would marry someone else. Unacceptable.

"I've changed my mind."

Of course, she may not want to marry him. In fact, having seen her blushing over Peregrine's hand, Jonah thought she might wish to scoop up Regina's discarded fiancé. Another reason to move quickly.

"It's Miss Valentine, isn't it? The woman you wouldn't allow me to dance with," Devin guessed, giving him a narrow-eyed look. "One dance, and you plan to marry her?"

"Yes."

"You always were decisive," his friend muttered. "I take forever to select a stickpin, and you take up any old thing and stick it in your coat."

"Choosing a wife is not like selecting a stickpin!"

"For one thing, Miss Valentine is not hanging around on your dressing table waiting to be picked up," Devin said. "You'd better start wooing. From what I hear, Argyle is making a claim."

Jonah frowned at him. "Do you think I should tell Miss Valentine that I can't hear on one side?"

"You're a bloody war hero," Devin said. "Tell her the cannon did in your hearing. Frankly, I would just dangle your ducal insignia in front of her eyes."

"She doesn't care." Jonah was certain of that. His only uncertainty was whether she'd hear his proposal at all.

Devin hooted. "There's not a woman in London who doesn't care."

Jonah shook his head.

Devin raised an eyebrow. "You'll have to seduce her, then."

"We're not all libertines," Jonah retorted.

"I know women, and I've heard a great deal of chatter about Beatrice Valentine. I presume you find her desirable."

Jonah gave him a look so ferocious that Devin threw his hands in the air and backed up. "All I'm saying is that you'll need to convince her of your feelings. That's all. My advice for what it's worth. I'm off to find my partner for the next dance."

Jonah walked over to his favorite wall and leaned against it, pretending that he didn't notice the people trying to catch his eye. He needed a campaign to win Beatrice's hand.

Seduce her? That was the action of a blackguard, a dissipated tomcat like Devin. He had to *court* her. With posies. Gifts.

Ladies popped up and talked at him, words burbling past his head in a steady stream designed to convince him of each speaker's adorable character, her cleverness, her wittiness...

Which only made him realize again that Beatrice Valentine hadn't been dazzled. In fact, he had the distinct impression that she didn't like him. After their dance, she hadn't shown the faintest interest in conversing with him. He almost had to catch her arm to talk to her at Almack's.

It was bemusing. He never had to start a conversation with a young lady; they'd always just drifted up to him and started talking.

Apparently, Beatrice Valentine didn't want to be a duchess. Or she didn't like him.

What the hell was he going to do about that?

He was wondering if he should pay her a morning call when his hostess, Lady Paget, popped up before him.

"His Majesty vomited on the billiards table," she said. "Then he passed out."

Jonah straightened. "Have you summoned his grooms?"

Prinny hired extra strong grooms for this very reason: they could lift his large frame as nimbly as if he were encased in an oak coffin and carry him off to his carriage.

"I'm having him removed through the side entrance," Lady Paget said. "I need you to rescue Miss Beatrice Valentine from the library and return her to her home in your carriage."

He froze.

His brain abruptly woke up. "She needs rescuing?"

Damned if he didn't nearly bare his teeth—which was the reaction anyone might have to the idea of a young lady being accosted. Or so he told himself.

"Surely you remember her. I heard you danced with her at the Sheffield ball," Lady Paget said. "Miss Valentine is a debutante like your sister, except she hasn't taken. She's the wrong shape and awkward in the bargain. There are rumors ... but then I never believe rumors."

Awkward? The way she danced was ...

Not awkward. Sensual. A woman who was centered in her body, who felt the music with every limb.

"Why does she need rescuing?" If some degenerate had touched her, he'd take him apart limb from limb.

Lady Paget blinked; savagery must have leaked into his voice. "Goodness me. I see that you *do* know Miss Valentine. I hadn't realized that you were more than acquaintances."

"We are not. Yet. What happened?"

"Nothing terrible," Lady Paget said. "She's had a sartorial mishap, and she must return home."

He bowed. "If you could ask her chaperone to—"

"That's just it," the lady interrupted. "Her chaperone returned home without warning."

Jonah's brows drew together.

"I shall have a talk with Lady Alcon about her dereliction of duty," his hostess promised. "Your sister stepped in when she realized that Miss Valentine had been stranded."

"Lady Regina has taken an interest in Miss Valentine," he said slowly.

"You could say that. Your sister offered Miss Valentine a place in your carriage. But unfortunately, the lady's skirts are drenched in water, and she needs to leave before the end of the ball."

Drenched in water?

"Miss Valentine cannot return to the dance floor," Lady Sheffield added.

The last piece of the puzzle fell into place with a satisfying click.

Regina had tossed water at Beatrice; he'd stake his estate on it. His sister's propensity to throw things had meant that no governess had endured their house for more than a few weeks, no matter what salary his father offered.

"One of my maids and a groom will escort her home, and then return in your carriage," Lady Sheffield was saying. "Miss Valentine is in the library. A footman will inform you when your carriage arrives, and I'd be grateful if you would escort her through the side door."

"Of course," Jonah said.

"Sometimes a girl just isn't suited for London society. She'll make someone a fine wife in the country."

Jonah pictured curvy Beatrice next to a tobacco-chewing farmer and didn't like it. She should be in ballrooms, her eyes filled with laughter, dancing like a feather.

"I don't believe she belongs in the country."

"With a vicar," Lady Paget said, with conviction. "Or a squire."

He was hardly an authority on young ladies. Perhaps Beatrice would love being immured in the country. If so, he had a big, rambling house she could fill with children. *That* he could see.

In fact, it was unnerving how easily he could imagine her bending over and holding out her arms so that a child—a little girl every bit as beautiful as she—could run into them.

"One of the maids will fetch a domino cloak for Miss Valentine to wear on the way home," Lady Paget continued. "Please remain here, Your Grace. You certainly don't want to be accidentally compromised by being found in the library with her."

"Certainly not," he agreed.

Dukes didn't have to obey commands. He'd never bothered to think about that truth, but the fact was he could do whatever he damned well pleased.

He could stay in the ballroom.

Or he could go to the library and find the sodden Miss Valentine. He could apologize for his sister's actions.

Or:

He could seduce her.

Chapter 12

After Lady Paget brought her to the library, Bea stood as close as she could to the fire until a maid appeared with a tray holding a pitcher of hot toddy.

"My goodness, you're drenched! You'd best take off those slippers," the maid suggested. "You might take off your stockings too, if you want. You won't be interrupted. Lady Paget told me that the Duke of Lennox's carriage will come for you in a half hour, but I'd guess it will be longer, as there's an awful crush in the street. Most of the guests are waiting for their carriages."

Bea blinked at her. "Already?"

"A number of them have cast up their accounts, and the Prince of Wales spewed all over the billiards table!" Her eyes were bright with excitement.

The library was peaceful and even more important, *warm*. The minute the maid left, Bea kicked off her slippers, untied her garters, and pulled down her sopping stockings. Her bodice and chemise were merely damp, but her skirts were still soaking wet.

She snuggled down on a comfortable settee in front of the fire, sipping the spicy toddy. She couldn't help smiling: One of the worst evenings of her life had abruptly become one of the best.

She had fought back. Stood up for herself.

Lady Regina's first attack, weeks ago, had been so unexpected and shocking that Bea had succumbed before she'd realized what was happening. By their third encounter, she began to feel short of breath at the very sight of Regina or her friends.

But now . . .

Regina had exposed herself in front of Lady Paget, a leader in society, which surely meant that she was unlikely to approach Bea again. What's more, Bea would never again be so vulnerable. She knew it in her core.

She had spoken back.

Regina loved to inspire fear and humiliation, which was why she created opportunities to shame Bea on the dance floor. Ironically enough, she had forced her brother into that dance at the Sheffield ball, which had led directly to Bea's salvation.

One single dance with a man who looked at her with a glow of admiration had given Bea backbone and made her remember that she was not merely a country mouse.

In the morning, she would begin preparations to return home, which would be a relief for poor Lady Alcon. Once back in Cheshire, she would inform her father that she meant to find a husband at a local assembly, because Londoners weren't for her.

Her heart lightened at the thought. She loved everything about Cheshire and there was still a month of spring left before the season—the *real* season—would turn into summer.

Query: What percentage of people invited to the Paget ball would choose a northwest county mostly known for its cheese over London?

Probability: Leaving her out of it, zero.

Not a single glossy aristocrat out there in the ballroom, circling each other while letting fly barbed remarks, would prefer Cheshire.

Though she did wonder about Regina's brother, the duke.

It might take a while to forget the burliness of him and the way he looked at her from shadowed eyes. She had loved dancing with him, but it wasn't until they'd talked—about barns of all subjects—that she truly noticed him as a man.

He wasn't as beautiful as Lord Peregrine. In fact, she'd describe him as striking, rather than handsome. His hair was mahogany dark and always seemed rumpled. He had icy gray eyes, the same color as Regina's.

Yet if Regina's were cruel, his were intense.

He had watched her from the side of the room as if he knew what she was thinking. Or as if he *wanted* to know what she was thinking.

He was bigger and bolder than she had ever imagined a husband. Her father was short and round, but she recognized a key similarity: like her father, the duke was, surprisingly, a hard worker. Clear-sighted, too. Bea had the distinct feeling that Jonah loved his sister dutifully, but without sentimentality.

He made her heart thump, but not because she was afraid of him, the way she was—the way she *had been*—of Regina.

Not that it mattered, since she was going home.

Lady Paget walked into the library, closing the door behind her. "I've prevailed upon the Duke of Lennox to allow you to return home in his carriage. He will escort you to the vehicle and inform his coachman."

"I truly don't want to put him to trouble! Lady Regina wasn't serious when she offered—"

"Oh, I know that," Lady Paget said, walking over. Her eyes drifted over Bea's slippers and the wet stockings draped on the fireplace screen.

"You might send me home accompanied by a footman, in a hackney," Bea suggested. "Or perhaps you could send a groom to my father's townhouse. Lady Alcon would send the carriage back for me. I'm sure she didn't realize that Lady Regina was merely funning."

"Lady Alcon ought to have known as much," Lady Paget said sharply. "Of course, I could send you home in one of our vehicles, in the company of a maid and groom."

"Well, then," Bea said, more happily.

"But I shan't." The lady turned her back to the fire. "Did you know that I was friends with your mother?"

"No, I didn't," Bea said. "As children, or when she was a young woman?"

"We were girls together," Lady Paget said. "I felt an acute loss when she died. I loved her very much. We exchanged letters every Tuesday for years, until we both had children, and life interfered. I must give you those letters. She writes about you so lovingly."

"I would like that of all things," Bea exclaimed. "I have memories of her, but they have faded, of course."

"How old were you when she passed away?"

"Eleven."

"Old enough to know what you have missed," Lady Paget said thoughtfully. "I have the odd sense that the duke might come to the library before his carriage arrives. Once His Grace sees your bare feet, he may consider himself compromised. Lennox is a man of honor, you know."

"Surely not!" Bea said. Toes—naked toes—could hardly be considered an indication of debauched behavior.

"Never underestimate the prurience of matrons' imaginations," Lady Paget advised. "Those ladies issue daily edicts regarding ladies' reputations—which have been lost for far slighter reasons than your state of undress. More to the point, don't you think it would be a satisfactory revenge if you scooped up Lady Regina's brother?"

"Absolutely not!"

"You don't like the duke?"

"No!"

"You sound like a bad actress, promising that she's not in love with the squire. You know what I mean," Lady Paget said, smiling widely. "A would-be nun, played by an absurdly pretty girl, who swears she doesn't want to marry the hero. Are you trying to tell me that Lennox hasn't bowled you over? I heard a rumor that he kept you talking in a corridor for twenty minutes."

"He was very kind."

Lady Paget snorted. "When he arrives, you can throw yourself into his arms and compromise him, or not, as you wish. I shall return to witness it myself. It's the least I can do for your mother."

"*What?*" Bea squealed.

"Compromise him," Lady Paget repeated, as carelessly as if she were talking about a morning call or a ride in the park.

"I don't understand."

"Kiss him," the lady clarified. "It would cause a marvelous scandal if you were caught in the act. Let's see." She glanced at the tall clock at the side of the room. "It's just past nine o'clock now. That blighted salmon pate has ruined Clarissa's debut, but a match between the two of you would eclipse my chef's sins in the eyes of society."

Bea would prefer that her marriage not be the result of bad fish paste, but she couldn't find the right words to express that conviction.

Lady Paget didn't wait for a response. "The duke will appear in a half hour. Don't let him take you directly to the carriage. I'll return at around ten, so fling yourself in his arms then, *if* you would like to be a duchess."

Bea straightened her spine and tried to look very resolute. "I have no wish to be a duchess, Lady Paget." Honesty caught up with her. "At least, not—"

The lady laughed. "Personally, I fancy the idea of you as Lady Regina's sister-in-law."

Bea shook her head and blurted out, "I can't think of anything worse!"

"You'd have the upper hand," Lady Paget pointed out. "Your mother would have liked to see you a duchess. But not, of course, if you've taken Lennox into dislike. When I was young…" Lady Paget said, a bit dreamily.

Bea waited.

"Well, I wouldn't have scoffed at a man with those shoulders. Especially if he was handed to me on a silver platter, title included. Have you taken a good look at his legs?"

"No," Bea said, untruthfully.

"He has a calf, unlike so many men out there," Lady Paget said. "I daresay you're the only unmarried lass in all of London who would refuse my offer. It's a pity, because a duchess has a great deal of power over society, and I think you'd make an excellent one."

Bea couldn't think of anything less appealing.

"You have your mother's figure, yet you don't take advantage of it. What a marvelous model that would be for young ladies. Forget leaping on him—that duke will leap on you, given the slightest encouragement."

"He will not!"

Lady Paget laughed, waggling her eyebrows. "You have much to learn of men."

Bea couldn't stop herself from asking: "Do I truly resemble my mother?"

"She was taller, but your eyes and mouth are your mother's, as are your curves. She had men fighting duels over her hand before your father won her heart. Of course, I could look about for another duke, in honor of your mother, but I must point out that there is an alarming paucity of them in London these days."

To Bea's mind, her mother would have been happy with any man who willingly offered for her daughter's hand—though not one whose proposal came about from a scandal born of bare toes, a salmon-paste dolphin, and a stolen kiss.

As soon as Lady Paget left, Bea walked back to the fireplace. She needed her clothing to dry out as soon as possible. Her bodice was merely damp, but her underskirts clung to her legs, no matter how she plucked them away.

The idea of compromising the Duke of Lennox was horrific. She wasn't that kind of woman. She had honor and decency.

But kissing him?

That she could imagine. He would hold her without hesitation, not like the one boy who had kissed her back home. He would pull her against his body until she felt the solid strength of his thigh—

Suddenly she realized there was someone in the room with her.

Chapter 13

*J*onah pushed open the door of the library.

Beatrice Valentine was standing to the side of the fireplace, staring down into leaping flames. Firelight bounced against skin that was the color of sweet cream with the faintest tinge of pink. Lips, dark rose. Eyelashes so long he could see them across the room.

Her lips made him think of the bedchamber. Oh, bloody hell, everything about her made him think of a bed, not just the room. Her skin was silky without even a freckle to be seen.

Perhaps that was one of the reasons Regina disliked Miss Valentine so much? His sister had weathered a case of measles that had left permanent scars. She carefully painted her face to conceal them.

Beatrice had tucked a few curls fallen from her topknot behind her ear. Her neck had a pleasing curve, though no gentleman would look below her collarbone.

He looked.

Her bodice wasn't as wet as her skirts, but it was damp, clinging to her chest. He could see a pert nipple that he wanted to lick and tease until she cried out. Cried his name. His big palms would wrap around her breasts as he brought them to his lips as if they were made for him.

Jonah was abruptly aware that his cock was high and hard.

He had to stop gaping at Beatrice Valentine.

This was terrible. Ungentlemanly in the extreme.

For the first time in his life, his body ignored his mind's command. Her skirts hugged her legs with loving attention except for a cloud of gauze that did nothing to conceal her limbs.

Or the cleft of her arse.

She was perfect. So delicious that his heart was thudding in his chest.

His hand tightened on the door, and he almost backed away into the corridor as silently as he'd come. He could send a footman in his stead. Then he imagined a man in livery gaping at Beatrice, and his heart drummed an answer.

Never.

He walked forward, closing the door smartly behind him, making his shoes thump on the uncarpeted floor. Startled, Beatrice pivoted to face him.

Their eyes met in one of the most intimate moments of his life. He was aching for her, on the very edge of losing control, and in that moment of madness, it seemed that she felt an equal bolt of desire.

Then she blinked. "Your Grace! Has your carriage arrived already? I thought a footman would fetch me."

"No footman is seeing you like that," Jonah growled. He'd never heard his voice with such a raw edge.

He kept trying not to look, but any man would imagine curling his hands around those luscious curves, cupping her lavish arse, pulling her up and into his arms. His hands wouldn't meet around her thighs, so he could take hold without fear of breaking her. The image of her laughing while waltzing, her mouth cherry red and sweet, merged with the idea of lifting her against his surging tool.

"Forgive me, Miss Valentine," he said, managing with an effort to sound civilized. "I see you are damp. May I offer my coat?" Without waiting for an answer, he wrestled himself out of it.

He felt unaccountably clumsy, as if he were wearing one of the tight coats Devin affected. He wasn't, but somehow the garment caught on his shoulders.

He must be drunk. He'd just neglected to swill brandy.

He stepped forward with his coat. "You needn't," Beatrice said, but she let him drape the coat around her shoulders.

"Someone might walk into this room at any moment. You mustn't be seen like this." He stepped back and dragged his hand through his hair. "The ball has come to an unexpected end. One of my grooms came to find me, saying that it will be at least an hour before my carriage manages to approach the front door. I thought I should let you know."

Beatrice's long eyelashes flicked as she glanced at a clock to the side of the room. "You should return to your sister, Your Grace. I would prefer not to travel home with Lady Regina. I shall take a hackney."

"Regina will be spending the night with Cecilia, Lady Paget's daughter. She and a group of friends have already retired to the upper floors."

Beatrice cleared her throat. "I would be more comfortable traveling with one of Lady Paget's footmen and a maid in a hackney."

He shook his head. "No."

"Why not?"

"You are my responsibility. Lady Paget explained that your chaperone left you to my care."

"Not that you had any idea," Beatrice pointed out. "Regina made that arrangement, not you."

"Also, you are wearing my coat."

"A maid will bring me a domino cloak. If you would simply return to—that is, go somewhere else, Your Grace, I would be very grateful. It is improper for us to be here together."

She was right about the impropriety. Her bare toes were adorable. That meant her legs were naked. Gossamer stockings were hanging before the fire, which struck Jonah as a shocking intimacy, as if they shared the chamber. His mind galloped ahead: if she was his wife, those delicate silk things would be part of his life.

He could spend hours rolling them down her legs and kissing every bit of her skin. Or he could leave them on, tied with a garter, but take all her other garments off. She would lie back against the bed, laughing at him, her thighs gleaming above her garters. Bending one leg so he could...

He took a deep breath and cursed himself silently.

Any other young lady would have taken advantage of the situation and sauntered over to him. Or was he being an arrogant ass, thinking every eligible woman wanted to marry him?

Beatrice wasn't making any effort to appeal. She had pulled the coat tightly around herself, so her bodice was entirely hidden, and she was frowning at him.

Jonah dropped into a chair.

Her brow puckered even more fiercely. "Why are you sitting down, Your Grace?"

"I've been standing all night," Jonah answered. Also, though he had no intention of pointing it out, she was wearing his coat, and his cock was tenting the front of his breeches.

Suddenly, like a storm coming in from the sea, she became truly angry. Her hazel eyes darkened, and she forgot to clutch his coat, which gaped in an interesting way at the neck.

A glimpse of Beatrice's breasts, even shadowed, was a gift.

"A gentleman doesn't sit down in the presence of a lady," she said scathingly. "Not unless he's a duke who thinks that he's better than a miss from the country. I cannot—"

She stopped.

"Cannot?" Jonah raised an eyebrow, feeling quite proud that he was keeping his eyes above her collarbones.

"You don't look as arrogant as your sister. No, that's not true. You *do* look as arrogant as Lady Regina. Obviously, you *are* as arrogant."

"I am arrogant, and so is Regina. Yet I have no intention of insulting you. I don't want to leave."

"Then I shall leave," Beatrice said instantly.

He glanced at the stockings and then back at her. "You will be most uncomfortable in wet garments. Won't you please sit down? I am trying not to look at your legs, though your gown is testing my resolve."

"Gown—" She glanced down at herself and then flew into the chair opposite him. At first, she sat properly, but after a second, she picked up her legs and curled her bare toes under her, tucking her wet hem around her feet.

Sadly, it wasn't appropriate to inform a young lady that her legs were exquisite. Was it possible to become inebriated from a woman's gaze? Hazel eyes that still weren't showing any obvious interest, but were potent as brady? Why the hell was that?

Maybe she had a man waiting for her at home, in the country. He could imagine a country squire's son lining up to dance with her. The lad would want to make her laugh. To inch closer to that magnificent bosom of hers. Perhaps close enough to be tempted to drop a kiss on her lips, because they were downright carnal.

The thought made him want to down a whole bottle of brandy.

"May I ask what you are drinking?" he inquired.

"A maid brought me a hot toddy," Bea said, nodding toward the tray. "With only one glass, which I am using. You may not ring for another. I don't want anyone to know you are here."

No one had ever looked at him with that expression. Mulish and condemning, and yet underneath he would swear that she was as dizzy with lust as he was. It was in her eyes.

"Are you smiling at me?" she asked suspiciously. "You apparently froze your expression into ducal solemnity years ago, so I'm not entirely sure."

"I'm not *that* old," Jonah protested.

"I agree that it is sad to see such rigidity at your age."

"I choose not to share my emotions." He reached over and picked up the jug. "You could think of it as shyness. Do you mind if I drink the rest?"

She wrinkled her nose—adorably, he noted once again. "I cannot imagine that you are shy. People want to be with you. They want to *be* you. Why would you be shy?"

Lennox upended the jug. Hot, spicy toddy slid down his throat, but the shock of it didn't seem to bring sanity. "'Shy' is not the right word."

"Churlish?" Beatrice suggested.

"A duke's every expression sparks interest, after which people make up reasons for the emotion they glimpsed. At any rate, I am churlish only when talking to impertinent young ladies."

Beatrice's eyes flashed again, and even though he ought to feel sorry for irritating her, he felt perversely pleased. He didn't want to see her cower, the way she had at supper in Almack's.

He'd seen Regina's petty cruelties have an outsized effect on people.

"I am not impertinent," Beatrice said, tilting her nose into the air. "You are so used to adulation that you don't know what normal interaction looks like."

"Truthfully, I have had almost no contact with young ladies." He put the jug down at the side of his chair. "After university, I went to war, and since my father died, I have been occupied with the estate. I am fairly good at talking to farmers."

She opened her mouth and shut it.

"I've had little contact with Regina, too," he clarified. "I'm seven years older than she, after all. By the time she arrived in the nursery, I had already been sent to Eton."

"Nonsense." She scowled at him. "Do you think I'm a dunce? Boys start at Eton at age eight or nine."

"Not if they're a future duke," he said, realizing that he kept telling her things that he wouldn't dream of saying in company. "We're expected to excel due to the power of the title. I began at six with a crop of eight-year-olds."

"That's—that doesn't sound easy," she said, her tone softening.

He shrugged. "I wasn't in the nursery when Regina was growing up, which was likely a good thing. I expect she would have used me as a chew toy."

She gave a surprised laugh.

He'd do a lot for that laugh, Jonah thought ruefully.

Damn it.

"It can't be easy being Lady Regina's brother," she said hesitantly. "She has very high standards."

He sighed. "Vindictive, malicious … feral. I promise that she won't bother you again. I apologize on behalf of my family."

Her lovely mouth rounded into a surprised circle.

"The moment I heard your garments were wet, I recognized my sister's propensity to throw water," Jonah confessed.

"I threw water as well," Beatrice said.

She frowned at his laugh, but then she giggled, and finally a clear peal of laughter sounded in the room.

"So, *you* dampened her petticoats," Jonah said, his voice rough. *Want*, pure *want*, was going through him like lightning or fire—a phenomenon that laid waste to the landscape and left space for new growth.

It seemed he was getting married.

She was his, and he was hers, even if she didn't know (or care, he thought uneasily).

It occurred to him that Lady Paget had informed him that Beatrice was in the library, knowing she was in *dishabille*. Knowing that if they were found together, especially if they were kissing, they would both be compromised. Knowing that the scandal would delight society for weeks to come.

Knowing that, as a gentleman, he would have no recourse but to offer his hand.

Interesting. It seemed he had an unexpected champion.

"My friend Devin insisted I give my sister a lecture on skirt-dampening," Jonah said.

"I merely sprinkled her gown with water." When Beatrice smiled, her eyes crinkled at the corners. When she was older, she would have thick white hair and laughter lines. She would be round and juicy and always desirable.

He smiled back, not bothering to hide his feelings.

"Stop that!"

"What?"

"Looking at me in an indecorous fashion," she ordered.

Jonah was having one of the best evenings of his life. The knowledge settled into his bones lazily, like the warmth of a bonfire after a day spent tramping through snowy woods. The corners of his mouth tipped up into a rare smile. "I can't help it. Tell me more about you. What you like to do."

"Do? *Do?* Your Grace, would you please return to the ballroom? I will send your coat back to you once I have a cloak to wear."

"Not until at least nine-thirty."

She glanced at the wall. "That clock just chimed the half hour."

It was to his left, so he hadn't heard a damned thing. "I couldn't possibly return to the ball without a coat, and I can't leave you here to be gaped at by whomever enters the room. What do you do when you're not in your father's barn?"

"Nothing that could possibly interest you. Won't you please leave?"

"No. I'm trying to court you, but I seem to be making you irritable instead. You do realize that I'm considered a catch on the marriage market, don't you?"

"I'm so pleased for you," she said, unenthusiastically.

He'd never asked anyone to marry him, but it seemed he was being turned down before he even proposed. Luckily, he was the sort of man who thrived when offered a challenge.

He was a born competitor; it was the basis of his relationship with Devin. The world that had dictated their birth had also dictated that they would face no friction. Everything handed to them on a silver platter: power, money, position. Women.

It was time to regroup and come up with a strategy, something better than a posy and a morning call.

"Go greet all your admirers, Your Grace," Beatrice said. "Why, I predict—"

"What?" He picked up where Beatrice stopped. "What do you predict?"

She fidgeted. "I think that there is a reasonable chance that you will marry one of your sister's friends."

"Do you count as one of her friends?"

Color surged back into her face. "That is not a kind question," she said, her hands curling into fists.

Damn it.

He was out of his chair before he realized what he was doing. Plucking her out of her chair. He turned around and set her on the library table and then stepped in, close.

New strategy.

Chapter 14

"Your Grace!" Bea gasped. He'd picked her up so smoothly, as if she were—well, as if she were a willow-thin girl.

Not *her*, with her hips and thighs and all the rest of her ungainly self. His eyes were fixed on hers. "Call me Jonah."

"I will never call you Jonah!"

"Why not? I will happily call you Beatrice. I think of you as Beatrice." He must have seen something in her eyes, because he said, "That's not quite right, is it? Beatrice is too formal, too Shakespearean. Beatrix?"

She shook her head.

"Bea," he exclaimed. "Bea, like a bumble bee."

Her laughter had a sardonic edge. "Small and round."

"Adorable, but with a sting," he countered.

His smile prickled the back of her neck. Adorable? "If I'm a bee, what animal are you?" Bea countered. "An eagle would be the obvious choice. Or a lion."

"I'll take a lion," the duke replied, unsurprisingly.

"Didn't you say that your name was Jonah?" She threw him a mischievous look. "We're not talking about a lion, are we?"

He raised an eyebrow.

"A whale," she said, enjoying herself. "Huge—because you are monstrously large, you know."

"I'm not huge."

"Enormous. Tall as a mountain, that's what I thought at first."

"Don't you like tall men?" he asked. No, he *growled* that question.

"Not much. I like people my size."

He bent his head, so close to her that she could smell the starched linen of his neckcloth. "Change your mind," he ordered.

She gave a stunned little laugh. "Aren't dukes supposed to be models of comportment?"

"I am," he said, adding, "Normally."

"It's not polite to ask a lady's preferences, or to order her to change them," she pointed out.

Something was sparking in the air between them like fireworks, silent but potent.

Jonah cleared his throat. "May I kiss you?"

The words hung between them. Bea's head was spinning. He couldn't really... He was Regina's *brother*! And he was a duke. An integral part of polite society. But he would never kiss her unless—

"I'm leaving London, returning home," Bea said quickly, before she lost her resolve. She was no duchess. He must be inebriated. The toddy had gone to his head.

"Is there a gentleman waiting for you?" His voice deepened, roughened.

Bea shook her head. "No."

Fascinatingly, his eyes changed color after her admission. "So, you love the country?"

"I do." She hesitated. "And you?"

"I frustrate my sister by missing meals and staying in the fields for as long as there's good light."

Bea lightly touched the muscles clearly visible through the light fabric of his shirt. "That's why you're so rugged."

He nodded.

"Why would you possibly want to kiss me?" she asked, unable to stop herself from blurting out that humiliating question. "Every young lady in Paget House, not to mention most of polite society, is enthralled by you. I have a game—" She broke off. "It's foolish."

"What is it?" He still hadn't taken his eyes off her face.

Bea wrinkled her nose, willing herself not to sway toward him and tip her mouth up for a kiss. She had the distinct impression that she didn't need to throw herself into his arms; she could simply look at his lips, and he would snatch her up. "You wouldn't be interested."

"If that were the case, I would not ask."

"You never lie?"

"I do not," he said evenly. "Though my father juggled lies as a matter of course, and Regina sees little profit in truth-telling. Tell me of your game."

"I use probabilities to predict the future."

He frowned. "How?"

Bea had the uneasy realization that she found his frown enticing, along with the bulk of him, standing between her and the door. Perhaps she did like tall men...even if they were standing far too close for propriety.

"I ask a question and then judge the probability of my answer. Using a percentage."

"You understand percentages?"

She scowled at him. "Your incredulity likely comes from the fact that ladies pretend to little or no knowledge. Pretense is not reality. My father is a banker. Of course I understand percentages, Your Grace. Just as I understand appreciation, dividends, and interest rates."

"My name is Jonah."

"Again, I'm not going to call you 'Jonah,'" she replied. "This is a very odd conversation. Please back up so I can stand again."

The duke ignored that request. "May I have an example of your game?"

"*Query*," she said, with a shrug. "What are the odds that the Duke of Lennox, a prosperous young man with all his teeth, could choose to marry any one of the hundred young women currently on the marriage market? Do you care to make a prediction?"

There were those sparks in the air between them again. Bea wasn't a woman who liked to surrender. True, he hadn't asked her to surrender, but it was there between them. The possibility. The allure.

"Just to clarify, I am predicting the accuracy of a query about whether I could marry any eligible lady whom I chose?"

Bea nodded.

"I would think my odds are fairly good. 100%?" His eyes were possessive ... even hopeful.

The thought made her dizzy. "No," she said, with a little snort. "Lady Martha is betrothed to an earl."

"You said 'eligible' young ladies. If Lady Martha is betrothed, she's not eligible."

The duke leaned toward her, and she smelled that whiff of sandalwood and clean linen that made her feel hot and muddled.

His eyes were on hers, serious and direct. "More importantly, I'm not certain that your father would describe me as 'prosperous.' If my lands continue to improve, I might earn the adjective."

A pang of sympathy went through her. Still: "You have lands. You are not destitute."

"You are right, of course. I think you should know that it will take hard work—*more* hard work—to bring my fields back to what they were before. At the moment, all my income goes to supporting the people who live and work on my lands."

"The right woman wouldn't care," she observed.

"She might want to come to London for the Season."

"She might not. She might think that she has more to give and more to do at your side." She was making a fool of herself. The look in his eyes made her burn with embarrassment. "Your Grace, you must allow me to stand up."

He instantly moved back.

"Who could have thought that I would give instruction in comportment to a duke?" Bea slid off the table to her feet. Her skirts were still wet. They hugged her legs, crumpled and damp, showing every curve and hollow.

Lady Paget must have been swallowed up in the turmoil of the vomiting guests, because no cloak had made an appearance. Bea would have to walk into the hallway without a domino.

Worse, with a duke walking beside her.

What if someone saw them leaving this room?

In a perfect world, the fact that a duke had been flirting with her would make her feel miraculously attractive.

But it didn't.

The drumbeat of Regina's scorn roared through Bea's ears, even given the fact that it was Regina's own brother whose eyes looked...

She didn't have the words. The right words.

Hungry? Her logical side utterly rejected that. Even if he was the kindest man in the world—and she was beginning to think that he must be—he couldn't be desirous. He liked the real her: she saw that. The side of her that was a bit ironic, somewhat serious, a little nervous, fairly courageous.

He was probably too "dukish" to laugh out loud, but he liked it when she laughed.

"What are you thinking?" Jonah asked.

"About how *dukish* you are," she said, blurting it out.

"'Dukish' is not a word," he observed.

"I apologize," she said, rolling her eyes. "I committed the cardinal sin of inventing an adjective perfect for the man in question. I think we're going to have to brave the corridor, you in your shirtsleeves, and me in your coat." She looked up at him. "Would you mind if I leave before you?"

"You would walk ahead of me ... *like that?*"

Her whole body jerked. His ... *like that* said everything. She glanced down at her plump thighs and fruitlessly pulled the fabric away once more.

"I understand," she managed. "Would you mind looking out the door and just making certain that no one will see us?"

A big hand pushed up her chin, and she met his narrowed eyes. "What?" he asked.

"Yes?"

"What did I say that was wrong?"

"Nothing!" she exclaimed. He was kind to the core, and how and why he was Regina's brother, she didn't know.

"Bea." His voice was dark and low. "I can't let you stroll down the corridor in that wet gown."

Heat was burning her cheekbones. "I know. I apologize."

"Apologize?" His hands closed around her upper arms. "For what?"

"I know, I just know," she whispered. "Please, can we leave it there? *Please?*"

His brows were drawn together. "No."

She realized that for Jonah, misunderstandings were like lies.

She stepped back, and his hands slid away. "I know that this dress is practically obscene, wet as it is," she said, head held high.

His head jerked but she kept going.

"I know that dampened skirts are…are disgusting, particularly when…Particularly when one has a figure like mine."

He stared at her for a moment, his brows knitted as if she were a puzzle he was trying to solve. "Your figure is not obscene. Did my sister tell you that?"

She tilted her head, indicating neither yes nor no. "I would prefer it if you left the room before me."

"No." His eyes roamed over her body. "Did Regina insult your figure?"

Bea groaned inside because the man was stubborn as…as a cow. "Yes."

"I've known she was mad for years."

"Well…"

He held out his hands, palms up.

Bea frowned at them and then looked up at his face.

"My fingers are trembling, Bea. Your curves, your body, your breasts, your hips are all perfectly sized for my hands. *You* are perfect for me. I look at you, and all I can think about is taking you to bed."

"Jonah!"

He leaned forward, eyes on hers. "I'm so hungry for you that I can't think straight. I keep telling myself to send you to a carriage, and then come by tomorrow with an appropriate posy and tell you some sort of compliment, but the truth is the only thing I want is to stroke you all over. Tongue you all over."

Bea was struck dumb.

He was looking at her as if she were desirable.

More than that: beautiful.

She blinked at him, and to her surprise, a low growl came from his lips. "What did she do to you, Bea? What did Regina do to you?"

"She was rude," Bea said, not caring much at that moment. She was too fascinated by the look in his eyes. She was about to take that last step toward him, slide her hands into his thick hair and pull him down to her—

She heard someone walking quickly down the corridor.

"I gather Lady Paget remembered the domino cloak," she said, glancing toward the door.

An expression passed through his eyes so quickly that she almost didn't catch it.

"They walked on," she said slowly. "Did you hear—"

He interrupted. "My carriage has surely arrived. I believe I'll go see if I can find my coachman."

"Of course," Bea said. She pulled off his coat and pushed it toward him.

His eyes fell to her breasts. She could feel herself growing red because they had bounced when she removed his coat.

"I'm not trying to attract you!" she snapped.

"You don't have to try, Bea." He was close enough so she could see faint stubble on his jaw. He stepped away before she could think how to answer, strode to the door, and walked out.

The clock began chiming ten o'clock. Bea leaned back against the library table, her knees weak with relief. They hadn't been caught together.

The door opened, and she put on a bright smile for Lady Paget. "I—"

It wasn't Lady Paget, or a maid with a domino.

It was Regina.

Chapter 15

"What are you doing here?" Bea blurted out. The wild thought went through her head that Regina meant to apologize.

Regina's hard gaze practically struck her in the face.

No apologies.

Jonah's sister sauntered across the room, her gauze skirts floating around her. *Her* skirts had obviously been pressed dry. "I want to give you a warning. And some information."

Bea nodded and crossed her arms, leaning back against the library table. "Be my guest."

She was gloriously unafraid. Why had she *ever* been afraid? This poker-like girl couldn't touch her.

"You may not take my brother."

Until that moment, Bea hadn't clarified the future for herself. She smiled. "Actually, I will. I plan to marry the duke."

Pure shock went through Regina's eyes. She'd been bluffing, trying to warn Bea off.

"I don't mean that the way Petunia did," Bea added, beginning to enjoy herself, just as Lady Paget predicted. "I truly mean it—whether Prudence has such an inclination or not. She can't have him."

"My brother hasn't asked you to marry him!" Regina's voice went up a full scale.

"Not yet." Bea let her smile widen. "We'll be sisters-in-law, Regina."

"You simply cannot!"

Her gasp, stiff shoulders, and curled fists caught Bea's attention. The problem here was Regina's, not hers. The girl was in a profound rage.

"Is this because you don't like my figure?" she asked with some curiosity. "You can't expect everyone to be as beautiful as you are." Regina had flaxen hair and a slim figure. She *was* beautiful.

Yet Bea was beautiful too. Curvaceous and *perfect*, according to Jonah.

"Don't smile like that!" Regina hissed, coming closer. "You can't have him. I never meant for the two of you to be in the carriage together."

"Actually, you are the reason why we found each other," Bea said. "Our first dance was at your instruction, and then you brought him to my table during supper, and finally you asked him to escort me home. He's gone to fetch his carriage now."

Regina's face went red. "I had nothing to do with it!"

Bea sighed. Hopefully, time would help them endure each other's company. "So, you came to warn me away from your brother. Is there anything else you'd like to say?"

"The duke needs a very different woman," Regina said. Her expression shifted. Suddenly she looked winsome, a little sad. "You don't know him. He has...defects. He *must* marry a woman at the very top of society. I'm trying to persuade Lady Martha to drop her fiancé and take my brother instead, out of the goodness of her heart."

"Defects?" Bea laughed. "Are those like my defects, the ones that Jonah likes so much?"

"Don't be disgusting!" Regina spat.

Jonah pushed open the door and froze. "What is going on here?"

A little sound escaped Bea's mouth. Not that she minded going head-to-head with Regina, but as Jonah strode toward her, his commanding frame—burly shoulders, thick, unfashionable thighs, big feet and hands—made her relax. He made her feel safe.

He walked past his sister and looked down at Bea, cupped one cheek, and dropped a kiss on her lips.

Bea stifled a gasp. She was compromised. Kissed in front of an audience, albeit a single family member.

"Are you all right?" Jonah asked, a husky promise in those words.

She smiled up at him. "Yes," she said simply. And again: "Yes."

"You cannot go ahead with this idiocy!" Regina erupted from behind him.

Jonah turned. "Why not?"

He wrapped an arm around Bea, but she stepped free. She had to stand on her own when it came to Regina; she couldn't let Jonah defend her, no matter how safe his looming presence made her feel.

"You have to marry someone *better*," Regina said, tight-lipped. "You know why, Jonah." She turned to Bea. "Our father was a degenerate who spent down the estate. My brother is practically a pauper, and he must marry someone with a huge dowry—a true fortune. Our family reputation needs to be mended in high society. His title is up for sale, and you're not good enough to be the Duchess of Lennox!"

Bea had already figured that out on her own. Luckily, her fortune was huge, but obviously, neither Jonah nor her sister knew. She grinned at him. "Perhaps we can auction off the title. What do you think, Your Grace?"

He looked at her, his dark eyes somber.

Regina burst back into speech. "You haven't even told her, have you? You don't think that Miss Valentine deserves to know the truth?"

Bea didn't like the expression on Jonah's face. He was at his most dukish, which suggested Regina's darts were injurious. "You should stop talking," she said to Regina, realizing with a jolt of delight that if Jonah made her feel safe, she could do the same for him.

Regina ignored her, of course. "If you marry *her*, you'll end up immured in the country, scything grain like a peasant. Never in London, never taking up your seat in the House of Lords!"

"You already know I won't take up my seat," Jonah replied. He was watching his sister with the intent look of a predator assessing a threat.

Bea shivered. Did she really want to be part of this family, or even worse, to come between members of this family?

"You must not lower yourself—"

Jonah's voice was deep, knife-sharp. "Be careful, Regina."

His sister narrowed her eyes. "You dare—"

"*You* dare." Suddenly he was far beyond dukish. *The* Duke of Lennox stood before them, enraged, the power of his ducal ancestors sounding in his voice as clearly as if ranks of noblemen stood at his shoulders.

Bea drew in a silent breath.

"I have done my best with you," Jonah stated. "I have tried, Regina. I don't know why you are such a calloused, unfeeling woman. If you were a man, I would have knocked you down long ago."

The room was silent but for the tick-tock of the grandfather clock. Patches of rouge showed on Regina's cheekbones.

"Perhaps you should have this conversation at a later date, when feelings are less high," Bea put in.

Jonah glanced at her with a warrior's rage in his eyes. Then they softened, and he nodded. Looking back at Regina, he said with precision, "You have shamed and disappointed me with your behavior for the last time. I will say this once, Sister: If you *ever* say an unkind word to my future wife, or any children we might have, you will never see me again. All England will know that the Duke of Lennox has repudiated his sister. Whose side do you think they'll take?"

"That's enough," Bea said.

"I've made my point," Jonah said, his voice suddenly casual. "I believe that you are staying the night with the Pagets, Regina?"

His sister nodded wordlessly, though her eyes were furious.

"I suggest you return upstairs. Your friends may be wondering where you are." His voice had a devastating twinge of disinterest.

Bea dropped a curtsy. "Good evening, Lady Regina."

Regina stood, head high, shoulders back. Her mouth opened but self-preservation prevailed. She wheeled about and silently left the room.

"Do you think that she will ever speak to me again?" Bea asked, not caring much. In fact, that sounded like an excellent solution to the impending problem of family Christmases.

Jonah shook his head. "Perhaps, perhaps not." He caught up her hands. "I will not allow her to destroy my family. I promise you that."

Bea gave him a beaming smile. She was without fear; she had a medieval warrior to protect her. Then she asked, "Jonah, did you hear the clock chime the half hour?"

A moment of silence, then he shook his head. "I'm deaf in the left ear from cannon fire."

Jonah met Bea's eyes with an effort. His gut tensed, waiting to see if she was as appalled as Regina had been by his hearing loss.

Her brows creased. "Is it better if I stand to this side?" She moved to his right.

"As long as I can see you, I can hear you. But if sound comes from behind, especially from the left, I miss it."

"I'm sorry," Bea said. She raised a hand, paused for a moment, and then put it on his chest.

Over his heart, Jonah noted.

Her light touch burned through his waistcoat and shirt.

"Thank you for your service to our country."

In recent years, Jonah had discovered that the world could be a very quiet place. At the moment, nothing existed for him but Bea's voice.

"In the North of England, we were terrified that Napoleon would invade," she continued. "We are so grateful to you, to all of you, who went to war and protected our shores."

"My regiment is still there, but I had to leave them." The truth fell from his lips. "My father died, so I had to come home, but even if that hadn't happened, without excellent hearing, I'm a danger to them."

Her fingers pressed lightly against his chest. "It must have been painful to leave."

"I know you don't want to marry a tall man, but what about a deaf one?" Jonah came out with it. "The doctors think there's a fair chance that I will lose hearing in my right ear as well."

Bea smiled. "You'll have to get used to carrying around foolscap so you can issue your dukish commands in written form, won't you?"

That smile in her eyes, on her lips, was genuine.

Regina had said...Jonah had discounted what his sister said, of course. But her hysterical insistence that he could not tell *anyone* about his partial—or impending—deafness had stuck to him in a greasy film.

"If I'm close enough to someone, in good light, I can read their lips." His voice rumbled from his chest. "I cannot manage the House of Lords. I can never take up my seat."

He had never seduced anyone. He'd never had to. Women fell into his arms if he so much as raised an eyebrow. Bea's lips were moving, but all he took in was *her*: a woman he wanted with a bone-deep certainty. His hands were trembling to shape her curves. He wanted to snatch her into his arms. He wanted to talk to her every day for the rest of his life.

If he caught her up into his arms, she might say "no," in which case, he'd have to put her down. Yet the expression in her eyes was desirous.

She didn't care that he might be deaf. She didn't care that he was a duke, either.

He didn't stop himself; he wrapped his arms around her, one hand on her back, the other cupping her rear and pulled her up so her breasts pressed against his chest.

Bea didn't say no; she cried, "Jonah!" with a laughing question behind the word.

The way she would say his name a million times over the years of their marriage.

"If I hold you like this, I can hear everything you say." He lightly ghosted his lips over hers. "May I kiss you, Bea. Please?"

That was her cue to refuse, but she merely looked at him, eyes wide, her lips parted slightly.

Jonah's tongue slid between her plush lips, and she tilted her head to the perfect angle. Her tongue danced with his, He poured everything into that kiss: hunger, respect, conviction ... *passion*.

Bea was intoxicating, her taste, her smell, the femininity of her. She wasn't frail and dainty. She was bursting with life and desire. Everything he ever wanted in the world in one irresistible person.

They kissed until she suddenly pulled back and said, "The time! Set me down, Jonah! Hurry. You can't be found here with me!"

"Why not?" But he put her on her feet.

"Because Lady Paget ... She—"

Jonah grinned. "She wants me to compromise you. I suppose she means to burst through the door, and shockingly discover you with bare toes? Your hair tumbling around her ears? Your lips puffy from my kisses?"

"Something like that," Bea confessed. Her hands caught his upper arms and she looked at him earnestly. "I don't want to have you just because of fish paste!"

Jonah's smile widened. She wanted him—though what fish paste had to do with it, he didn't know.

"Do you want to marry me?" She groaned and stepped back. "I can't believe I just said that!"

"You know damn well that I want to marry you," Jonah growled. "When do you think I last kissed a young lady?"

She narrowed her eyes. "I don't want to know. I was brought up in a moralistic household, not a noble one. You might want to reconsider the proposal you haven't made, if you think you could fall into bed with any woman other than your wife." She started. "I can't believe I said that!"

Jonah threw back his head and laughed. "No extramarital congress. No congress with anyone but my unladylike wife," he teased. He picked her up again and kissed her.

She gave in, submitting to him, kissing him back. His erection was painful, the head of his shaft throbbing against her.

"Now *that* is ungentlemanlike," she murmured.

Jonah pulled back just enough to see her eyes. "Will you marry me, Beatrice Valentine? Will you be mine for now and always? When I'm doddering and deaf?"

"A doddering, deaf duke," Bea said, teasing him, her eyes shining. "I'm not sure."

He kissed her again, hard and deep. Then: "I'm not a great bargain, title aside. My lands are depleted. My close family consists only of Regina, and she's not a good person. The dukedom brings trouble with it."

"But you come with the title. We can work on your lands together. I have a dowry. A big dowry." Her arms were looped around his neck. She leaned forward and rubbed her nose against his. "Weighing the two against each other…"

He had a knot in his throat.

"*Query,*" she whispered against his lips. "Will Miss Beatrice Valentine accept the Duke of Lennox's proposal, even though it comes with a title and an irritable sister?"

He swallowed. "Prediction?"

"100%." She kissed him again. "Yes, Jonah, yes."

Chapter 16

The Duke of Lennox's carriage was very grand indeed: a barouche drawn by four black horses, their reins the same dark crimson as the body of the coach, the side painted with a coat of arms featuring a black lion, a few dogs, and—

Bea squinted. "Is that a unicorn?"

Jonah looked down at her, sardonic amusement in his eyes. "We Lennoxes are proud of our ability to lure virgins."

"Jonah! Hush!"

Luckily no one was in earshot except Lady Paget, who had followed with one of her maids.

"There's a tangle of carriages in the city tonight," Jonah's coachman reported, placing a mounting box in front of the carriage door. "Could be as long as an hour before we reach Miss Valentine's address, Your Grace."

"Take a route around Whitechapel," Jonah told him, turning back to talk to Lady Paget.

Over Jonah's shoulder, Paget House blazed with candlelight, not giving the slightest indication that behind its golden windows, elegant persons were vomiting fish paste. On the other side of the street, a line of graceful mansions loomed against the dark sky.

As Bea looked up, the clouds parted, and the moon seemed to shake free of a curtain. All of a sudden, the roof opposite was graced with a weathervane, a four-sailed clipper floating over velvet-dark skies, silver glinting from the tops of its masts.

In comparison to the country, Bea considered London foggy, ever-darkened by a relentless cloud layer. But tonight, she could see a star or two, and the huge bulk of the cathedral loomed comfortingly over the city. London had its own glittering beauty, albeit very different from the gentle country life she adored.

Marrying Jonah, becoming a duchess, would mean spending time in London. She could make her peace with it.

"One of Lady Paget's upstairs maids, Elsie, has kindly agreed to accompany you home, Bea," Jonah said, ushering forward an older woman with a beaked nose and cheerful eyes, her round forehead ringed by a thick braid. "Lady Paget would be grateful if Elsie could stay the night and return in the morning."

As Jonah escorted the maid to his carriage, Bea curtsied to Lady Paget, who twinkled at her.

"You didn't obey me, child. I was about to come to the library when the duke came to find me."

"No," Bea said. Then her smile broke free. "No need."

"I had a delightful feeling that my interference may not be required. I thought of informing the duke that I'd ask Lord Peregrine to escort you home instead, but decided the prompt was not needed."

Bea shook her head. "You are mischievous, Lady Paget. I wouldn't have thought it."

"I do like to get my own way," the lady said with satisfaction. "My husband complains of it regularly. Though I must say that Lady Regina casts me in the shade on that front."

Bea's heart thumped. It was only nerves. In time she would hear Regina's name and have no more reaction than she did to hearing news of the family cat. "Oh?" she managed.

"I'll leave it to her brother to share the lady's latest machinations," Lady Paget said. "Nothing too terrible, dear. She's a tiresome little gnat. There's one in every family."

After saying farewell to Lady Paget, Bea accepted Jonah's hand to climb onto the mounting block and into the carriage, holding tightly to the cloak covering her damp clothing. The vehicle was lit by small lamps hanging at each window, creating a snug little room braced against the cold and dark.

She didn't know London well, so she found herself puzzling over Jonah's instruction to the coachman: Why go around Whitechapel?

And why did Lady Paget call Regina a "gnat"? Because she's a small insect that buzzes around one's hair, yet is harmless? Was her ladyship trying to reassure Bea, or merely expressing irritation?

After a few final words to their hostess, Jonah jumped in, pulling the door shut and seating himself beside Bea. "Are you comfortable, Elsie?"

The maid grinned. "Believe me, this is a fair treat, your lordship. The household's been scrubbing hard for two hours. The number of guests heaving up Jonah is mad."

Jonah—who was so close to Bea that their legs were touching— broke into a rumble of laughter. "A reference to the Biblical vomiting whale?"

"All the pails of hot water that's gone up the stairs already! The scrubbing and the smell! I'm plumb exhausted. I hope you won't mind if I rest my eyelids."

"Of course not," Bea said warmly.

Before they turned the street corner, Elsie was tucked in the corner, a brown wool cloak pulled over her head.

"I can scarcely believe the tales of woe emerging from the ball-room," Jonah said. "We were lucky to have been upstairs and avoided the fishpaste."

"Actually, I should thank your sister for that."

Jonah raised an eyebrow.

"I stopped eating food at balls because she would mock me," Bea told him.

His brow drew together. "I shall speak to her again. I apologize for her unkindness."

"Lady Alcon holds to the same rule," Bea said. "What if a spot of grease found its way onto a lady's gown? One should never eat in public."

He picked her up and popped her down on his other side. "I hear you better on this side."

"I will remember," Bea told him.

"I'd like to say that I didn't hear what you just told me, but I did."

The look in his eyes would have made her shiver if it were directed at her. Bea decided it was a good time to change the subject. "If you don't mind my asking, why did you route the carriage around Whitechapel? Isn't that east of my father's house?"

"It is." He took her hand and began to pluck off her gloves. "I wanted time to talk to you."

She squinted at him. "Not to seduce me?"

"In a carriage?" He looked astonished, as only a duke can do. Presumably, His Grace did not often encounter surprises. Then, with a deep chuckle: "In the presence of our chaperone?"

The slight whistle of a truly exhausted sleeper was emerging from under Elsie's cloak.

"I always wanted a lusty wife," he added, a wicked glint in his eyes.

Bea's insides tightened with a mixture of desire and embarrassment. "Jonah! I am a very proper young lady!"

His hands curled around hers, his eyes holding her gaze. "I have bad news on that front."

Her stomach tightened with embarrassment. Had he realized that every time she looked at him, she wanted him to kiss her? That even a glance at his thighs made her feel hot and muddled? He was ravishing her with every glance.

"I'm afraid that everyone already believes I've seduced you in the library."

It took a moment for his words to sink in. Bea's heart sank. "That's impossible! Lady Paget would never share unpleasant gossip."

"Regina was in a rage, and she took her revenge. Lady Paget just informed me that every guest who isn't too busy vomiting into a chamber pot believes that I had my way with you."

"*Regina* compromised me?"

"My sister is claiming that our marriage was entirely at her behest, right down to the 'accidental spillage' of a glass of water on your gown that immured you in the library, vulnerable to my conquest."

"But Regina doesn't want you to marry me! And isn't she impugning her own brother's reputation by claiming you seduced me?"

"My sister is forthright, if vulgar. I've seen similar behavior from the Prince Regent," Jonah said. "She declares the world to be as she views it, and astonishingly often, people agree with her depiction."

"I do see what you mean," Bea said slowly. After all, on encountering Regina's conviction that she, Bea, was disgusting, she had agreed with that characterization herself; she'd accepted a version of reality that she *didn't* believe, and certainly didn't like.

"On the other hand, she's known me her entire life, so she understands that I've made up my mind and her opinion will never change it," Jonah continued. "She seems to think that I'm at your feet, Bea. You must have given her the impression that you intend to accept my proposal."

Bea bit her lip, remembering that conversation. She cleared her throat. "I did."

"She snatched that triumph from my hand by making it her decision rather than mine."

Her heart sank. "Do you mind terribly?"

His mouth slowly tipped into a smile. "I don't give a damn what she says or thinks. Nor anyone else either. I did not seduce you in that library." His eyes brimmed with desire and mischief, a combination she never thought she'd see in the haughty duke. "We haven't had extramarital congress. Yet if you would allow me, Bea, I'd love to amend that oversight."

"Jonah!" Her eyes rounded.

"Not at this exact moment." He glanced at Elsie.

"I am not interested in dalliance," Bea said, turning up her nose.

"Neither am I, at least, not for its own sake. When I was in France, during the war, I didn't lie on my pallet thinking about fornication, to be blunt. I imagined finding a woman like you. A woman who would laugh and love and make a family and a home. You're incredibly beautiful, but you are also funny and kind and brilliant, and that matters so much more."

"Well, you're gorgeous too," she managed. "A hard worker. Oh, and a duke and all."

A dark chuckle. "You don't care about that."

"True, it's a liability in the balance sheet. And your sister—" Bea stopped there.

Jonah tipped up her chin and brushed his lips over hers. "I will protect you from Regina."

"I know, but she's a member of your family. More to the point, *why* is she like that, Jonah?"

"Like what?"

"Mean," Bea said. "'Mean as a worm,' my grandfather would have said."

Jonah turned over her hand and examined her palm before putting a swift kiss in the middle of it. "She was born that way."

"No one is born that way," Bea protested.

"Yes, they are." Shadows accented his lips and his cheekbones: sharp-cut, beautifully shaped. Aristocratic to the bone.

Bea instinctively put her free hand to her lips. They were as puffy as the rest of her. He was all hard angles and aristocracy. She was ... Well, she was a country banker's daughter, never mind her mother's claims to blue blood.

"You really shouldn't touch your mouth like that," Jonah said conversationally.

She instantly dropped her hand. Was that a society edict? One of the rules that Lady Alcon had meted out sprang to mind: *Don't eat in public, in fact, don't eat at all.*

"Your lips are too damned beautiful," Jonah growled, learning forward so the sound barely stirred the air between them. "If you draw my attention to them, I won't be responsible, chaperone or no."

"Oh," Bea said. She smiled at him, but still: "Your sister."

He shifted restlessly. "There's no revelation I can give you, Bea. I can't point to the moment when my sister decided she was an arbiter of society and began passing judgment on those who didn't meet her standards. It just happened. That silly girl, Martha, didn't help. Her mother is one of the patronesses of Almack's."

"Regina tells lies," Bea said flatly. "It isn't true that you seduced me in the library. Someone who tells lies like that, about her own brother, wouldn't hesitate to do it again. That's dangerous, Jonah."

"Only if one listens to her." He caught up her hand again and bent his head, his lips dusting hers. "And we shan't. We'll live in the country as much as we can. You'll like the estate, Bea. There's a nice hodgepodge of buildings, with an old stream running through the meadow at the bottom of the back gardens."

"That sounds lovely," Bea said.

"I've a house here in London too. Bigger than Paget House, and in better shape, since we renovated it for Regina's debut. I put in water closets."

It occurred to Bea that perhaps Jonah's report that he wasn't prosperous might have been exaggerated.

"Would you mind if I kissed you, Bea?" His voice was casual, as if he were suggesting a cup of tea. When she didn't say no, he dipped his head and licked her bottom lip. His hands went to her shoulders and pushed the domino cloak away.

Bea's mind clouded, and she leaned toward him, wrapping her arms around his neck. "More," she whispered in his ear.

"My lady's wish is my command." He picked her up and placed her in his lap.

Bea's blood was on fire with longing. She shifted against him and felt . . .

Hmmm.

Jonah's lips parted, and he groaned. Before she could say anything, he began kissing her, holding her tightly while his tongue swept through her mouth, firing her blood.

She wound her arms around his neck and leaned in, letting her breasts rub against his chest.

"Damn it, Bea," Jonah said, his voice needy and dark.

She came to some sort of dim understanding in the purplish twilight of the carriage, with no sounds other than Elsie's deep breathing and the clatter of carriage wheels.

Regina wasn't important.

Jonah *was*.

Yet there was still time to step back, to take a breath, to say no. A logical, insistent voice in the back of her head kept making that point over and over. She had never had the ambition to be a duchess. She certainly never wanted a sister-in-law whose own brother described her as "feral."

But there was Jonah, leaning toward her, his eyes fierce, his head tilted slightly to the side. Already she recognized that tilt, an instinctive bend toward sound he wanted to hear. She wouldn't be surprised to see him tilt his head the other way in Regina's presence.

He would never be an easy husband: never compliant, amenable.

Jonah wasn't *placid*.

He swept through the world with a ferocious need to change it. He might have inherited that characteristic from the powerful dukes who came before him, those who commanded private armies and hundreds of serfs.

Or it might just be an intrinsic part of the man before her—the man who was on his knees, metaphorically at least.

Something he was born with, just as Regina was born with a temper.

She leaned in, and he kissed her again.

They were fierce, longing kisses, the kind that skirted the edge of impropriety. Jonah's hands hovered and then landed warmly on her breasts. Her hand ran up his back but didn't pull on his shirt.

Elsie slept on.

Chapter 17

In later years, Lady Alcon remembered the aftermath of the Paget ball as one of the most unpleasant periods in her entire life. It began when her breakfast was spoiled by an offensive note sent to her by Lady Paget. Thereafter, she experienced shock after shock, most of them disagreeable.

"If Lady Paget sends in a card, I am not at home," she informed the butler, sweeping past him into the drawing room. "Where is Miss Valentine? Go upstairs and inform her that punctuality is an essential quality in a lady. She ought to have been in the breakfast room at least a half hour before I arrived."

Then suddenly she remembered that she had directed Beatrice to stay away from the breakfast room, in hopes that it would inspire her to slim down. Instead, Lady Alcon had the strong feeling that the housemaids simply fetched the girl whatever she wanted, feeding her in her bedchamber.

Perhaps even in her *bed*, which was permissible only for married ladies, not that Beatrice would ever be one, unless her father bribed a farmer to wed her.

That thought spurred her irritation even further. "Go on!" she said, flapping her hands at the butler. "I swear that girl is as lazy as a toad at the bottom of a well. I'll have tea, but don't bring anything other than dry rusks unless we have a morning caller. Close the door! And don't forget that I am never home to Lady Paget!"

Seating herself in the drawing room, she moodily returned to thinking about that horrid letter. Who was Lady Paget to question why a charge was sent home in an eligible duke's carriage?

Other chaperones would have gnashed their teeth to achieve that situation!

Those chaperones didn't have to marry off a plump country girl who likely fell asleep in the carriage and ignored the duke altogether.

The butler opened the door. "Lord Peregrine."

Never in a million years had she envisioned the richest man in London paying them a call. Lady Alcon sprang to her feet and hurried toward the door. "Lord Peregrine, what a pleasure." For a dizzying moment, she thought the bunch of violets in his hand were for her. Stranger things had happened—

"I trust that you and Miss Valentine avoided the illness of last night? I brought her a small posy," the gentlemen said, handing his violets to a footman.

"I've always heard that Lady Paget keeps an unclean kitchen," Lady Alcon said spitefully. "At any rate, neither of us partook in the fish paste." Behind his back, she saw her butler frantically waving a footman up the stairs to fetch Beatrice. "My rule that no true lady partakes of food in public kept us safe."

Lord Peregrine's eyes skated over her body, but surely she had mistaken his indifferent expression. She was very proud of having kept her girlish figure. If she wished, she could still don gowns from twenty years ago.

"Miss Valentine will join us in a moment!" she said brightly, leading him to a settee. "How is your dear fiancée, Lady Regina?"

"No longer my fiancée," he drawled.

He was a truly unpleasant man. The way his lips curled? No wonder Lady Regina had discarded him.

"Young girls are quick to change their mind," she said, trying for a consoling tone. What was taking Beatrice so long?

"Miss Valentine played a signal role in freeing me from that imprudent betrothal," Lord Peregrine said coolly. "I thought the least I could do was to offer my gratitude in person."

Lady Alcon choked back a startled comment.

Thankfully, Beatrice had finally hoisted herself out of bed. The butler opened the door, announcing, "Miss Valentine," and then, without pausing, "The Duke of Lennox."

In the second shock of the day, Beatrice was smiling up at the duke as if they were the best of friends. Apparently, she didn't sleep in the carriage.

Lady Alcon quickly looked the girl up and down. Beatrice had put on a low-cut morning gown in a cornflower blue that emphasized her creamy skin. She did have an excellent complexion.

Those abundant curves couldn't be hidden, but since some men are susceptible to melon-sized breasts, she had done her best to advertise them. After all, that was all Beatrice Valentine had to offer, other than her dowry.

"Damnation," Lord Peregrine said, perfectly audibly.

Lady Alcon startled, having forgotten him. He was staring at Beatrice with an unmistakable admiration in his eyes. It seemed both the duke *and* Lord Peregrine admired unfashionable curves.

He muttered something else, using even more reprehensible language.

"You dare curse before a lady?" Lady Alcon snapped, before she could stop herself.

Lord Peregrine ignored her, striding toward the couple standing by the door. "Miss Valentine, Lennox," he said, bowing. Beatrice dropped into a curtsy. The duke merely nodded.

As Lady Alcon watched, feeling as if she were in a theater rather than a drawing room, Lord Peregrine caught Beatrice's hands and brought them to his lips. To his lips! She had never seen him make such a romantic gesture toward Lady Regina.

The way he was smiling down at Beatrice?

It should be outlawed. In fact, she had the feeling it *was* outlawed, at least in polite society.

It wasn't until the duke stepped forward and calmly removed Beatrice's hands from Lord Peregrine's that the truth dawned on Augusta Damaris Alcon.

She had done it.

One of her charges was about to become a duchess. *She* had arranged the most significant match of the Season, one that would be chattered about for a decade.

A flash of pure gloating glee went through her. After this Season, she would be the most desirable chaperone in all London, with her choice of all the available debutantes. She could invoke standards: no country maids, obviously, and only those with slender figures.

What's more, she could charge double what she'd charged Mr. Valentine—frankly, she had taken advantage of his ignorance as it was.

She simply had to make certain that the marriage actually went through. Clearly, the world had changed since she was a girl. She had the distinct impression that Lord Peregrine had extracted himself from his betrothal to Regina, something that would have been inconceivable twenty years ago.

Lady Alcon sprang into action. First, she had to get rid of Lord Peregrine, in case the duke was irritated by the presence of competition. He might well leave of his own accord; surely, Peregrine understood that a huge fortune did not trump a duchy. Second, she would send a groom with an urgent message to Beatrice's father. Finally, and most importantly, she had to make certain that the attachment the Duke of Lennox seemed to have formed turned into a proposal.

When she reached the three of them, she was glad to see that Lord Peregrine didn't have that deadly look he got when he was displeased.

He turned to her with a bow. "It seems that Lennox stole the prize while my back was turned. I shall bid you good morning, Lady Alcon."

Beatrice was blushing prettily; Lady Alcon had to admit that she was attractive, in a full-figured sort of way. Hopefully, one fleshy duchess wouldn't start a fashion.

"Thank you for paying us a call, Lord Peregrine," Beatrice said, curtsying.

Luckily, he made his way out the door without waiting for a cup of tea.

Lady Alcon turned to the Duke of Lennox. He did not share Lord Peregrine's faintly amused air. Instead, Lennox wore a primitive, masculine expression that was somewhat alarming. She began blinking rapidly. "Your Grace, it is a pleasure to see you this morning." She sank into a deep curtsy.

He bowed. "I have asked Miss Valentine for her hand in marriage, and she has agreed. Perhaps you would be so good, Lady Alcon, as to write a message to Mr. Valentine requesting his immediate presence in London?"

"Certainly," she said, gasping a little. "As soon as we have tea, I will—"

"Now," His Grace stated.

That one word made Lady Alcon remember just how glad she'd been—after the grief, of course—when Lord Alcon passed to his just reward, hopefully Heaven.

"Jonah," Beatrice said, as if she'd known the man for years.

He caught up her hand and kissed it, but kept his eyes on Lady Alcon's face, which was most uncomfortable.

"I intend to marry your charge immediately, by special license. I compromised her last night, after you deserted her."

"I—You—"

"You left your charge at a ball, with no provision for her safety nor way to return to her own house. Without so much as a farewell." His eyes drilled into her.

"Lady Regina . . . " she faltered.

"My sister is a feckless and unkind girl, who had no intention of telling me that Miss Valentine had been left under my care. Since you did not bother to inform me or Miss Valentine, your charge would have left to make her own way home from the ball."

Beatrice cleared her throat. "I would have safely returned home in a hackney, Jonah. I believe Lady Alcon wanted the best for me."

"I did!" Lady Alcon chimed in.

The duke's chilly composure didn't warm an iota. "For your sake, Lady Alcon, I hope that Mr. Valentine paid you in advance, because I doubt he will be pleased by my account of your chaperonage."

"Well, I never!" Lady Alcon gobbled. "That's . . . You're . . . "

Beatrice took her arm. "Don't worry, Lady Alcon. You can depend on my recommendation. But perhaps it would be good to write to my father immediately. I am afraid that most of London does believe that something imprudent happened between myself and the duke last night."

Lady Alcon's heart sank. It was one thing to chaperone a young lady who married a duke with pomp and circumstance, preferably in a cathedral. It was quite another to have two charges in a row marry in a hurly-burly fashion by special license. This wasn't quite as bad as the elopement of last year, but very nearly.

"Meanwhile, I shall bring my fiancée to meet my uncle," the duke announced. "He is currently attending the Prince Regent, so we will not return until the afternoon."

Lady Alcon swallowed. She would have loved to accompany her charge on rounds of celebratory visits, puffing her role as chaperone, but the duke couldn't have made it clearer that she was excluded.

The image of her sister's charming cottage in Devon popped into her mind. Polite society wasn't as welcoming as it used to be.

Hardly knowing what she was doing, she scuttled through the door, her heart pounding. She would write to Mr. Valentine, of course. But she would also write to her sister.

Bea put her hands on her hips. "You mortified that poor woman!" she chided, frowning at her future husband.

Jonah looked completely unrepentant. "Would you want another young lady to go through what you did? Starved on a daily basis, and then deserted at a ball?"

"No," Bea admitted.

"She should never have left you last night. Anything could have happened."

Bea didn't want to ruin her good mood by fretting. "It is true that you could have seduced me—but you didn't." She drifted closer and put a hand onto his chest. "Did you know that my parents eloped?"

"Dukes buy marriage licenses and do the thing properly in the family chapel," Jonah informed her.

"All right." Bea leaned in. "You haven't kissed me good morning."

His eyes instantly darkened. "No more have I." He bent down and gave her a fierce kiss, but rather than pulling her closer, he drew her out of the house and into his waiting carriage.

Bea didn't hear what Jonah told his coachman, but she had a good idea that it didn't involve a direct passage to wherever the Prince Regent was. In the subsequent long minutes of kissing, she found herself nestled on the wide seat.

Watching, as Jonah tore off his coat. Smiling, as he unbuttoned his waistcoat. Gasping, as he pulled his shirt over his head.

"Do you trust me?" he asked.

She had to tear her eyes away from the way his shaft was outlined by his breeches. "Yes."

He bent over and then straddled her on the wide bench. "*Query:* Will the Duke of Lennox marry Miss Beatrice Valentine, and live with her happily, in sickness and in health, as long as they both shall live ... whether he seduces her before marriage or not?"

"That's easy," Bea murmured, looking up at Jonas's beautiful eyes, realizing that she didn't just like this big burly duke.

Somehow, he had walked into her heart when she wasn't looking. She reached up and pulled him down to her.

"*Prediction:* 100%, Yes. Yes."

Chapter 18

Jonas's chest was rough with hair, corded with muscle. A working man's body, a soldier's body.

Bea took in a shaky breath and reached out to touch him, learning that his body jerked if she touched his nipple, that his lips parted in a groan if she stroked her fingers down to his waistband.

The carriage was a warm nest, one that swayed gently. It felt natural to pull down her bodice, to allow Jonah to undo her stays.

Jonah's wild eyes when he saw her breasts? She would never again feel shame or embarrassment at their size. To him, to her future husband, they were perfect. His huge palms could indeed have been made for the express purpose of caressing her, shaping her, delighting her.

Rough thumbs, used to manual labor, rubbed her nipples, and Bea dropped all pretense of ladylike behavior, squirming toward him, desperate for his touch, for his weight.

"I want you," Jonah said, voice hoarse. "Bea, may I have you?"

Bea had only one worry. "What if we reach your uncle's house, and the footman opens the door, and there we are?"

A smile curled her duke's lips. "I told my coachman to drive about until I banged on the roof and gave him further directions."

Bea laughed, the sound hanging in the air as Jonah pulled back and stood up, bracing one hand against the roof as he toed off his shoes, pulled down his breeches and stockings. Then he stood over her, one hand still above his head, and let her look her fill.

She was aching at the sight, her blood racing, aroused in a way that she had never experienced before. The feeling smothered any qualm she had about supposedly maidenly behavior. She reached out and let her fingers sweep down the hard, thick length of his tool.

His eyes were hot and longing, looking at her.

At *her*.

She had to stop ogling the heavy planes of his muscled chest and pay attention. "Is this real?" she whispered.

Jonah bent over, kissed her hard on the lips, and then crouched beside the bench, hands shaping her waist, pulling gently at her gown. She lifted her hips and her skirts slid away. Her chemise followed.

"From the moment I first saw you, I pictured this moment," Jonah said, hoarsely, his hands caressing the tender skin above her garters. His eyes were devouring her every curve, and there was nothing in them but desire. "I'm not sure this is real. I imagined your legs, your thighs, but I couldn't have known how plush they were, how soft your skin, the way your garters... And then there's *this*."

His fingers slipped up the curve of her thigh to the silky tangle of hair. "I never pictured how miraculous you are, Bea. Not just you, your body, but the way your eyes are laughing at me."

He closed his eyes and took a breath before saying, "I feel greedy and selfish. It's as if everything I ever wanted in life is here, in the carriage."

"Come here." She tugged at him. He came up on the wide seat, knees braced on either side of her. "You don't think I'm too plump?" She hated saying the words, but she forced herself to ask.

His eyes showed frank disbelief. "Look at me, Bea."

She giggled. "I am. I have been."

"Do I look like a man who wants to make love to a woman with legs like a dragonfly?"

"A *dragonfly*?" She choked and started laughing.

"You know what I mean." His hands were all over her, adoring her, sliding beneath her and squeezing the curve of her arse. "I can worship every inch of you, without worrying whether you'll break like a twig." He lowered his voice to a growl. "I'm going to go hard, Bea, and you—you'll love it. You'll be with me every inch of the way."

Bea swallowed because she didn't know exactly what he meant, but she instinctively welcomed it. The ragged tone in his voice told her that the curves of her belly and breasts and thighs set him on fire.

"I imagined *this*." His growl stilled as his hands swept again over her breasts, her middle, her generous hips, her curving thighs, a thumb dipping between them. "You're so wet, so luscious … What man wouldn't? But I want *you* even more."

Bea was dizzy with joy. And desire. A wild mixture of both things at once. "Let's make love," she whispered, eyes on his. "Now. I'm seduced. I promise I am."

"As am I," he whispered, his voice rumbling in her ear. Finally, finally, he moved so that his warm body came down on hers.

Bea's legs naturally slipped around his hips, and she gasped. His weight settled on her. He was right: they were perfect together.

He propped himself up on his elbows and kissed her until she couldn't help wiggling restlessly under him.

"If my father is coming to London, and you're insisting on a marriage license, this is your only chance for extramarital congress, Jonah." She gave him a mock frown.

He laughed again, his voice deep and husky. "You're perfect, do you know that?"

She did. In that moment, as the love of her life gave her a possessive, desirous look? As he caught her arse in one of those huge hands and put her in just the right position? As he filled her with pleasure?

She knew.

"I love you," Jonah growled.

The words were true and deep, coming from his soul and his heart. Bea went up in flames, because making love was too beautiful and too *perfect* to speak.

Which meant that long minutes later, when he finally stopped thrusting and gave one final shove, filing her to the hilt, driving her to ecstasy and making her cry aloud …

She cupped his face, still panting, and said "I love you, Jonah. Duke."

"My duchess," he said on a groan, his gaze burning into her. "I will love you forever."

For a time, they lay tangled up with each other, enjoying the way the carriage offered a mimicry of the fiercer motion they had just created on their own.

"I can't believe you seduced me in a carriage." Bea said sleepily.

A moment of silence, and then Jonah said, "Carriages are like stables, Bea. The sound is easy to separate. There's the street outside versus the space inside. I can focus on you and hear every moan, every word, every cry."

"So, are you saying that there are other long carriage rides in my future?"

"If you will allow."

She dropped a kiss on his shoulder.

Jonah was pretty sure she didn't mind that idea. In fact, he meant to buy one of those new-fangled carriages: the ones where one seat slid under the other and the whole thing turned into a bed.

Cheshire was a big county with much to explore, after all.

"I can't wait to take you to my estate," Jonah said. "Do you suppose that we could go directly after the ceremony? It will take approximately three days."

Bea was lying half on top of him, the gentle pressure of her breasts against his chest, bringing him halfway to arousal again. It might be a lifelong condition, he thought, and tightened his arms around her.

His was the joy of the cat who found the cream, the whale after expelling Jonah: the most simple, base pleasure of the body.

"I don't even know where your estate is!" Bea said, a pang of surprise sounding through her sleepy voice.

"Cheshire."

Her head popped up. "Truly?"

"Truly."

She rubbed her cheek against his chest. "You are the perfect man for me. I'm from Cheshire, and I love it. Tell me about the duchy. That's the right term, isn't it?"

Jonah ran a hand down her back. "The main building is medieval, with a cobbled courtyard, but lots of Lennoxes added their bit in years after. We have a turret, and a cupula, and even a cloistered interior garden, with a walkway that runs through a string of pillars. Great Tudor chimneys that stand out against the sky when it's not raining. Eight of them."

"It sounds fancy."

He thought she sounded alarmed, so he let his careless caress turn warmer, fingers curving around her hip, assuring her that there was nothing fancy about him and his farmer's hands. "Not really. There are coats of arms every place you look, but most of them were badly carved by local workmen. A couple of the unicorns look like pigs wearing admirals' hats. There are stone cornices over the windows, each of them topped with a rampant unicorn. Most of the horns have broken off, so they look like stallions with three ears."

Bea kissed his neck. "Fancy stallions."

"I suppose it might have been fancy once, when it was first built. But now it's a working house. The windows in the front don't face pleasure gardens or a long winding entrance. They look onto fields, wheat and sugar beets, though a very clever person told me that I should try clover, so I mean to switch crops. Instead of stately elms, we have gnarled horse-chestnuts."

Her lips slid up his jaw, and she nipped him.

Jonah was no longer half-erect but throbbing and stiff again. He eased her up his body until he could see her face. "Are you in pain?"

Bea's hair was tousled around her face, and her lips were bee-stung with kisses, but she wrinkled her nose at him and laughed. "Don't be silly. You know exactly how I feel. I told you."

"You did, didn't you?" He kissed her. "There's a marsh to the west that turns purple with heather and then gold with gorse. Some of the buildings have fallen down—the granary and the buttery, for example. Maybe we can mend them someday."

"Beer doesn't appeal to me, so I don't care about the buttery, but how is the creamery? For me, cheese is close to divine."

"The creamery is thriving," Jonah said smugly. "Turning out a Lennox variant from a recipe going back to 1530. We have special cellars, and we deliver to hotels as far away as Congleton and Macclesfield."

"Red, white, or blue cheese?"

"Red, of course." He snorted. "The others are *nouveau* pretenders, dating back a mere hundred years or so."

"I can see that I'll have to spend time teaching you that the modern age is here. I love blue Cheshire."

Jonah had no complaints about that. She could do as she wished. "The barns are big and as old as the main house, made of stone that has stood the test of time."

"Like you," Bea said.

"I'm not old!"

She had her elbows propped on either side of his head now, so she could kiss him between sentences. "You will stand the test of time. You went to war, Jonah, and you came back here, to us."

"That wasn't my choice. I mean, I wanted to, but not all my men managed to return," he said. "Local lads, most of them. We *all* wanted to come home. My childhood friend—" He broke off.

"What was his name?" Bea asked.

"William Edward Stanhope. Or just Ed. He was brilliant. He was going to go to Oxford and study philosophy, but the war came."

She kissed him again. "You were together?"

He nodded.

"I didn't mean to say that men didn't want to come home from war," she said, tracing his bottom lip with one finger. "I simply meant that some people go through life without connections, weightless. You have all these responsibilities, and you've come through. You're coming through. I'm proud to marry you."

Jonah never cried—well, only once, when Ed died in his arms—but he felt that warning prickle in his throat now. This bright-eyed woman would go through the rest of it, the rest of life, with him. Next to him.

"I'm proud to marry you too." His voice was rough.

Bea grinned at him. "Remember what I told you about my dowry?"

He scowled at that. "We'll put it in a trust for the children. I've no need of your money, Bea."

"It's not *my* money," she said, kissing him. "It's *our* money."

Damn it. The prickle was a little harder to choke back; Jonah couldn't help comparing what Bea was saying to Regina's declaration that her dowry would belong to *her*, and never mind the laws of England.

"Don't you want to know the size of my dowry?"

He shook his head. "We'll save it for the younger children. My lands are entailed."

"No, we won't," Bea said impudently. "Remember how I told you that my father delighted in the stock market, gambling on the prospects of foreign companies?"

"Yes. You rope in his more extravagant ideas."

"When I can. But we are both fascinated by predictions," Bea told him. "Between us, we've made a lot of bets—'probabilities,' we'd call them—that have worked. Mine more than his." She couldn't suppress her grin.

Jonah's brows drew together. "What exactly are you saying, Bea?"

"My father informed Lady Alcon that he would give me a respectable dowry."

"I just need you, not your dowry."

"But the money that I made myself, figuring out percentages and putting money behind my bets?"

"No..."

"Oh, yes," she said with satisfaction. "*Query*: if the Duke of Lennox marries Miss Beatrice Valentine—and he'd better, because he debauched her in a carriage—will he be able to rebuild all those outbuildings, add a cupula or two, and still found an Oxford College, if he wants?"

Jonah was distracted. "Why would I want to do that?"

"Oh, I thought perhaps in honor of Ed and his love of philosophy. But it wouldn't have to be a college. We could build a chapel or create a scholarship. So...your prediction?"

Jonah knew that if he tried to put into words what he was feeling he would lose control. He would say unmanly things and perhaps shed unmanly tears.

Instead of speaking, he turned over his precious soon-to-be wife and kissed a lingering, possessive trail up and down her body, lavishing her with the feelings that he wasn't good at putting into words, but which she seemed to understand without a problem.

"Won't your horses grow tired?" Bea whispered, sometime later.

Jonah grunted.

He was lying beneath her, which was good because there had been a moment when Bea thought she might stop breathing from the pure weight of having a man the size of a house on top of her.

She smiled to herself.

She had thought she was broken by Regina's cruelty, but that wasn't true. She had been cracked and forged again, stronger, like double-glazed china. Inside, she was herself again, the girl who'd spent hours playing in the stables and never considered herself pudgy or any other unpleasant word.

Because she knew she was loved.

And lovable.

That was the saddest truth of this whole Season: Regina wasn't lovable and somewhere underneath it all, she knew it.

"I suppose I should bang on the roof and send us back home," Jonah said, his voice husky. "Damn it, woman, you've exhausted me. Stripped me to the bone."

Bea reached out and caught her chemise, then sat up and pulled it over her head. Not to cover herself up, because her soon-to-be husband loved every inch of her, every dimple and every valley.

But because she would like a hot bath. Her hair was tangled. She was thirsty and sweaty. She poked Jonah.

"Humph."

"Bath, tea, toast," she told him.

He opened his eyes and looked at her, his gaze sliding from her face to her breasts. His shaft, lying quiescent on his belly, stiffened.

Bea laughed.

"Lifelong condition," Jonah said, putting his hands behind his head, which made his muscular chest look particularly desirable, emphasizing the washboard effect of his stomach.

"Up," Bea said. "Bang on that ceiling."

"If we do that, I'll have to give you up. Lady Alcon won't let me spend the night with you."

"Very true," Bea said.

"I refuse." Jonah grinned at her, a wicked joy in his eyes. "I'm the duke. I think we should drive all night."

Bea sighed. Her duke had a lot to learn: for one thing, he didn't seem to know much about a lady's need for a chamber pot. She got up on her knees and gave the roof a thump.

A little door slid open. "Yes, Your Grace."

"Back to my house," she shouted.

Jonah pulled her back down onto his body. "Your first command as a duchess!"

Bea couldn't stop herself from running her tongue over his bottom lip. "You don't know where we are in London, do you? I mean, how far we are from home?"

He tipped open the velvet curtain. "A half hour at least." He reached out and positioned her on top of him, pushing up her chemise so that . . .

Bea heard her own voice, throaty with desire and love. "Was there something you wanted, Your Grace?"

"You."

Epilogue

Seventeen years later: 1832

The Lennox Townhouse, London

The Duke and Duchess of Lennox's ball in honor of the debut of their eldest daughter, Lady Sophia

*L*ennox Mansion sounded like the backstage of a theater before opening night, what with the clatter of people rushing here and there, musicians practicing their best waltzes, the occasional clash of cutlery echoing up the stairs.

The Duke of Lennox's elder daughter, Lady Sophia, in whose honor her father's ball would open the Season, stood before a tall glass, swishing back and forth, examining herself from head to toe.

Her pale lemon-colored gown was cut in the very latest fashion, low over her magnificent bosom, with voluminous sleeves and a tight waist marked by a large buckle. She wore one curling feather in her hair, and diamonds in her ears.

Bea thought her daughter was utterly exquisite and was certain the polite world would agree.

"You're making me dizzy flouncing about like that!" Sophia's younger sister Lucy called from where she was curled up in a chair to the side, reading. "You're getting frightfully vain."

"No, I'm not," Sophia retorted. "I'm just excited—doubly excited—because I was supposed to come out last year, and then of course my debut was delayed when poor Aunt Regina died. We've been in blacks for so long."

"Blacks were too good for her," Lucy muttered, not for the first time.

"Lucy," Bea said in a warning voice.

"I'm sorry, Mother," Lucy said immediately. "It's just that Aunt Regina wasn't very nice to us, was she? Remember when she advised Sophia to drink nothing but barley water for two whole days before she was set to debut. Can you imagine?"

Bea smiled ruefully.

Regina had never lost her conviction that a true lady is without curves, although in more recent years, she had disguised her opinion as advice. More importantly, Bea's girls loved their curves and always responded kindly to "poor Aunt Regina," whose husband had run away after just a few months of marriage.

"I know, I know," Lucy said, sighing. "She is responsible for bringing you and Papa together, so we owe her everything. But you must admit, Mama, that Aunt Regina wasn't always kind."

"She didn't just give you a mother and father," Bea pointed out. "She gave you a new brother, as well."

Lucy hopped up and came over to the rocking chair, peering at the little boy in Bea's arms. "Reggie is sweet, isn't he?" she crooned, kissing his cheek. "Even if his mother named him after herself!"

No one was certain where Regina's husband had gone—fled to the moon, Jonah had suggested to Bea—but in his absence, Bea and Jonah were raising Reggie. The babe had been born early, after his mother caught the infection that took her life. He struggled for the first few months, but now, at a year, he was thriving.

Even thinking of the first month of Reggie's life gave Bea a chill, so she kissed him on the forehead, admiring his sweet, chubby cheeks and rosy lips.

"That boy is being kissed to death," Lucy commented, before she followed suit and kissed him again, too. "Thank goodness, he's finally growing some hair. That bald look might work for a monk, but not for an eligible young man."

"He's hardly eligible yet," Bea said. She hated the idea of her children leaving the nest, though she knew perfectly well that Sophia was standing on the edge, eagerly looking out at the world.

"Mother, do you think that I should wear one more feather in my hair?" Sophia twirled. She paired her mother's figure with her father's confidence. She was a beauty, and she knew it.

"I think you are perfect as you are," Bea said, smiling at her.

"As are you, Duchess," a deep voice said, as strong arms curled around her shoulders from behind.

Jonah and she adored their children, as a tribe and singly. But Jonah was her heart. With luck they would grow old together, holding grand-babies, still loving each other.

Bea tipped back her head. "I didn't hear you come in."

"That's my line," he said, grinning.

Thankfully, the doctors had been wrong, and Jonah retained hearing in his right ear. All the same, the two of them loved nothing better than sitting together in a quiet barn where Jonah never wondered if he should be listening for something other than his beloved wife's voice.

Or taking a carriage ride.

He reached down and tapped the baby's cheek. "Reggie is looking well, isn't he?"

"A bonny lad," Bea said, rubbing her cheek against her husband's arm.

"Hopefully he'll be better behaved than our son and heir."

"What's William done now?" Lucy asked.

"He poured a bottle of my best cognac into the punch," her father said.

"Naughty! I might have become tipsy!" Sophia said indignantly. "I could have missed steps. As it is, I'm worried about dancing the *Varsouvienne*."

"*Query*: What is the chance that Lady Sophia, after three years of dance classes—not to mention that dance tutor who had to be let go with a broken heart—will turn the wrong way during the *Varsouvienne*?" Lucy demanded.

"30%," Sophia said.

"Nil," Lucy retorted. "They will all think you the most elegant lady on the market. If only all those gentlemen knew you the way I do!" Then she shrieked and put her book over her head in defense as Sophia dashed over and started batting her with a fan.

"Will's been sent down from Oxford again," Jonah told Bea.

His wife grimaced. "That boy is not meant for academic life. The good thing is that it will be hard for them to expel him from Lennox College, founded by his very own papa, won't it?"

Jonah shook his head. "Actually, I think they will take delight in that particular expulsion. He'll be all right. Will has a good idea about investing in a steam locomotive. Shall I take the baby to the nursery? I know he's a sound sleeper, but this squawking might wake him."

Sophia and Lucy were trading alliterative insults, a family tradition as beloved as the art of prediction.

"Blithering barnacle!" Sophia cried, pointing her fan at Lucy.

"Pissy provincial," her little sister retorted.

"I am *not*! This dress is from Paris!"

"Sassy saucebox!"

"Pooh!" Sophia said, turning back to the glass.

Bea allowed Jonah to pick up the baby and then stood herself. "I suppose I ought to begin dressing."

Her husband looked at her, a wicked twinkle in his eyes. "I could help you dress."

"I heard that!" Lucy squealed.

But her father was kissing her mother fiercely, and she knew from experience that they hadn't heard her. Her father had an excuse; they'd all learned to move to his right side if they had something important to say.

But her mother?

When she didn't want to hear, she just didn't listen. And she never wanted to listen when they were kissing.

Lucy sighed and went back to reading.

Printed in Great Britain
by Amazon

42021093R00078